MATT DAMON

When he was sixteen, Matt was signed by an agent in New York City after using money he had earned by doing a T. J. Maxx commercial to travel to the audition. A few years later, he was appearing in made-for-TV movies with legendary actors such as Robert Duvall and Tommy Lee Jones.

While studying at Harvard University, Matt started writing the one-act play that would evolve into the screenplay for *Good Will Hunting*. The hit film earned nine Academy Award nominations, including a nod for Matt's lead performance. In March 1998 Matt and childhood friend Ben Affleck won the Oscar for Best Original Screenplay.

With major roles in several upcoming films, Matt's star is definitely on the rise! But what's this boy from Boston really like? What's in store for him now that he's conquered Hollywood? And could *you* be the girl for him? Read all about *your* favorite leading man:

MATT DAMON

Look for other celebrity biographies from Archway Paperbacks

MATT DAMON:
A BIOGRAPHY

MAXINE DIAMOND
WITH
HARRIET HEMMINGS

POCKET BOOKS

New York London Toronto Sydney Tokyo Singapore

An *Original* Publication of Pocket Books

POCKET BOOKS, a division of Simon & Schuster Inc.
1230 Avenue of the Americas, New York, NY 10020

ISBN: 0-671-02649-6

First Pocket Books printing July 1998

10 9 8 7 6 5 4 3 2 1

POCKET and colophon are registered trademarks of Simon & Schuster Inc.

Front cover photo by Gallo/Retna

Printed in the U.S.A.

For Helene Diamond

The author wishes to acknowledge the contributions of these people: Lisa Clancy, Liz Shiflett, and Julie Komorn, at Archway Paperbacks, for their encouragement; Greg D. for his tireless support and excellent suggestions; Marcus B. for his exclusive tips; and Sean O. and Anna H. for all their countless hours put into the researching of this book.

CONTENTS

MATT DAMON:
A BIOGRAPHY

INTRODUCTION

Fighting through the throngs of admirers and press, it took Matt Damon forty-five minutes to walk down the red carpet at the Los Angeles Shrine Auditorium, as fans, who had camped out the night before, yelled for him and screamed his name. It was a big night: the 1998 Academy Awards. Who could have guessed that a script he had started six years earlier in a college writing class would have taken him to this point. But what a fitting end to a long, bumpy road. And how cool was it to have gone through it all and shared the sweet success with his best friend, Ben Affleck. Life can't get much better.

His success does not come as a surprise, though, to anyone who knew him as a youngster. Even as a child, it was obvious to those around him that Matt would be an actor someday, and most likely a very famous one. From his early play-acting activities through children's theater, and expanding into more mature roles in high school, he committed himself body, mind, and soul to each character he played.

Every step of the way Matt was supported by his family, friends, and teachers. From an early age, Matt's mom, Nancy, who raised him in a communal-type household, encouraged him to use his imagination while creating make-believe characters. Gerry Speca and Larry Aaronson, high school teachers who directed him in many a play, would let Matt mold his roles as he saw fit. And while he was at Harvard he was able to hone his acting and writing skills even further. From these inspired beginnings, Matt's career has soared ever since his one line in his first film, *Mystic Pizza*. But with the success of *Good Will Hunting*, this is just the tip of the iceberg for him. Matt has a long career ahead of him, one that will probably see him winning more awards for writing and acting for many years to come.

Matt Damon's story is one of hard work, guts, imagination, and love for family and friends. His commitment to his art can only compare to his loyalty to those closest to him, whom he cherishes and who keep him grounded. So, as Matt's star continues to shine brighter and brighter we can expect nothing less than good will and good performances from him. But to understand where he is now, one needs to take a look back and see where he came from.

1

MATT DAMON,
NBA SUPERSTAR?

He may not be a math genius, but Matt Damon is probably more like the character of Will Hunting than you might think. He grew up in Boston, had a college sweetheart named Skylar, has been best friends with Ben Affleck since they were kids, and has even overcome a fair share of obstacles on his way to becoming one of the biggest silver-screen stars of today. Not to mention that he's genuinely a good guy, liked and respected by most everyone with whom he comes into contact.

Life began for Matthew Paige Damon on October 8, 1970, in Cambridge, Massachusetts, a suburb of Boston and home to Harvard University and MIT, where *Good Will Hunting* is set. The comparisons to the abused and abandoned Will end, however, when it comes to his parents. He was born to the ever-supportive Nancy Carlsson-Paige and Kent Damon, who met while both were attending Syracuse University in Syracuse, New York, and married in 1966. Nancy is a professor of early childhood education at Lesley College in Cambridge, and Kent is a retired investment banker. Matt's parents split up when he was two years old, because, as Matt told E! Online, "My dad had this *Leave It to Beaver* idea of how life should be, and it just didn't work out." Though they've been divorced for more than twenty years, Matt's parents have remained in close, friendly contact. They have even been known to celebrate their "non-anniversaries" together. In 1991, on what would have been Nancy and Kent's twenty-fifth wedding anniversary, the whole family—Matt, Nancy, Kyle, and Kent—went out to dinner to celebrate. When the waiter asked if they wanted wine, his dad said, "Of course, it's our twenty-fifth anniversary." The waiter then turned around and announced it to the whole restaurant. Matt's dad stunned the patrons of the place into silence by explaining that actually they had been divorced for the past nineteen of those twenty-five years.

After the marriage ended, Nancy moved Matt and his brother, Kyle, who's three years Matt's senior, to another suburb of Boston called Newton, a quiet middle-class area that is said to be one of the oldest suburbs in the country. By the time Matt was born, Nancy had very clear ideas as to how she wanted to raise her sons—as thinking, imaginative individuals. She is, after all, a professor of childhood development. She has even written several books on kids learning violent behavior from watching cartoons and playing war games, including *Who's Calling the Shots? How to Respond Effectively to Children's Fascination With War Play and War Toys*. So, in essence, Matt and Kyle were banned from playing with war toys and sitting in front of the TV watching cartoons. As an alternative, she let them use their imaginations to create their own make-believe worlds using whatever methods appealed to them, from play-acting to blocks. Nancy's nontraditional techniques influenced her boys' futures probably more than she intended: Matt's dramatic play inspired his successful acting career, and his brother became a sculptor. Thanks in part to his mom's shrewd guidance, Matt was on his way at an early age.

Not that anything was going to hold him back anyway. His "second father," Jay Jones, who is also a teacher at Lesley College, recalled the day that a determined young Matt decided that he was ready to give up his beloved pacifier. As the garbage truck pulled up to the house, Matt stubbornly marched outside and heaved it into the truck himself. In another act of supreme confidence (and a bit of actor's fantasy) Matt one day decided that he was the superhero Shazam. Wearing his blue cape (a bath towel around his neck), he leapt from the top of a jungle gym, accomplishing the awesome feat of breaking his ankle. He was four at the time.

Nancy, always concerned about her boys' education, started to realize that her sons didn't like their elementary school in Newton, and therefore weren't going to be learning much. Nancy says that "mornings were agony" for Matt and Kyle, who were unhappy in Newton, especially in school. "Matt used to hide under the kitchen table wrapped in a quilt each morning before school," she told the *Cambridge Chronicle.* Heeding Matt's somewhat strange warning signs, she decided to move her two boys back to Cambridge, where, she felt, the school system was better.

So when Matt was ten, his mom and her partner Jay Jones bought into a broken-down house in Cambridge's Central Square with five other families, many of whom were also working in the educational field. A commune-style house might have raised a few eyebrows had it been in Kansas City, but in Cambridge, Massachusetts—hippie in an East Coast, academic sort of way—the living arrangements fit right in. All of the families had their own apartments, but there was a shared living-room area, and if someone needed something fixed, anyone who was available would help. As Matt told *Vanity Fair,* "It [the household] was governed by a shared philosophy that housing is a basic human right. Every week there was the three-hour community meeting, and Sundays were workdays. My mom put little masks on me and my brother, gave us goggles and crowbars, and we demo'd the walls." Growing up in this type of community environment full of interesting characters had positive effects on Matt's creative development. "It was a great way to be raised, especially for an actor. Lots of different perspectives, just surrounded by lots of positive human beings," he said.

It was during this time that Matt met Ben Affleck, who would later become not only his best friend, but his acting and writing partner as well. It was inevitable that the two would meet—they only lived two blocks apart. It's not for certain, though, *how* Matt and Ben actually met, but it is agreed upon that they met when Matt was ten and Ben was eight. The stories of their initial introduction vary from their mothers being the go-betweens to their meeting on a little league field (Matt's even boasted about striking Ben out a number of occasions). But one of the best stories, as recounted by Ben's little brother, Casey, is that the two met while in jail. Well, not exactly. According to Casey, they met while on a school field trip to a jail, no doubt as a lesson and reminder of what happens to convicted criminals. They wound up being put in the same cell. They hardly needed the jail house experience to teach them a lesson though, they were already extremely good, drug-free kids; Ben has even said that Matt was the type to bring his teachers apples.

Though Ben was already acting professionally when he met Matt, the acting route was not as immediate a realization for Matt as it had been for his best friend. Ben, who had been exposed to acting as a kid (his dad was involved in a Boston theater group when Ben was growing up), started working as an actor almost from the time he and Matt first met. In his first professional gig in 1981, Ben was cast as an eight-year-old visiting the

Mayan ruins in a PBS production called *The Voyage of Mimi*. He even appeared in an after-school special at fourteen called *Wanted: The Perfect Guy* opposite Madeline Kahn. But Matt wasn't as clear about his thespian aspirations. At the time they met, Matt's first obsession was basketball, and he practiced seven or eight hours a day. He had visions of the NBA dribbling in his head. That dream ended abruptly, however, when his father told the then twelve-year-old Matt, "You know, your favorite basketball player, 'Tiny' Archibald, is called Tiny because he's only six-feet-one-inch tall." With a new perspective on size—his father is the tallest Damon at five-feet-eleven—Matt decided to rethink his future. He made a good decision.

Though we could thank Matt's dad, who lives in Boston's posh Back Bay neighborhood and to whom Matt's very close, for that early intervention, it came as no surprise to Matt's mom that acting was his calling. Nancy says that she could tell from the time he was two what destiny held for him. She says that he was into "dramatic play and that he would be a famous actor some day" and that even at eight years old he was clear about his future. "He ran in and said, 'I know what I'm going to be when I grow up,' and I thought, 'So do I,'" Nancy told the *Cambridge Chronicle*.

But Larry Aaronson, one of Matt's high school teachers and a longtime friend of the family, thinks that maybe Matt's brother, Kyle, had an influence on Matt's acting penchant. "Matt's brother was an actor and a dancer and even a comedian in high school," says Aaronson. "Matty wanted to be like his brother."

Regardless of what influenced and inspired him, once he made his decision, Matt threw himself into acting with as much energy as he had put toward basketball. He started taking pantomime and other types of acting classes. And while he was in grammar school at the former Cambridge Alternative Public School, he performed in children's theater at the Wheelock Family Theater in Boston. But it wasn't until during his high school and college years that he was really able to put his talents to work.

2

STAR POTENTIAL

HIGH SCHOOL YEARS

The Big Money (and Big Hair) '80s were just getting into full swing by the time Matt became a teenager. Lots of people were making lots of money in the stock market. Ronald Reagan had just been reelected to a second term. Kids wore button-down polo shirts and penny loafers to school. And they were just starting to listen to, and watch, their favorite stars—Michael Jackson, Billy Idol, and Madonna, to name a few—on a brand new cable television channel known as Music Television or MTV.

This was Matt's world as he entered Cambridge Rindge and Latin high school in 1984. He was chosen to participate in an alternative program there called the Pilot Program. It was considered highly radical at the time, encouraging diversity as well as creativity. The students even got to make up some of their own rules and were on a first-name basis with their teachers. Matt was always a good student, with a special knack for writing. But ironically, unlike his character Will in *Good Will Hunting,* Matt struggled with math. Because he had already given up on basketball, he wasn't involved in the school's organized sports teams anymore, although he and his buddies would play pickup basketball from time to time (which he still does today when he can spare a free hour or two). As you might expect, he was a popular guy, and as Casey Affleck told *People,* "He was the guy who sat in the back of the bus always making out with his girl-friends." But his first love was always acting—he even thought of himself as a bit of a drama geek.

It was during high school that his acting started to mature from children's theater and mime to a more serious craft. He was thirteen now and start-ing to play parts that required a bit more subtlety than, for instance, the character of John John in a spoof of the cheesy '70s TV show *The Waltons.* But even as he turned the corner into his all-important teen years, he never got "too cool" to let anything get in the way of his devotion to acting. His enthusiasm never waned—he attacked his new roles with the same energy he had as a young superhero. One of his first stage roles at Cambridge Rindge and Latin was a samurai in a Kabuki play. "He was this little dervish, running around, re-hearsing his part, all his moves, making sure every-thing was just right," said Matt's drama teacher Gerry Speca, who was his first major acting influ-ence.

According to a classmate, Matt was usually cast as the lead in school plays, such as in the musical *Guys and Dolls,* a New York story about gangsters and gamblers. Even at this early age, his confidence to tackle a wide range of roles became apparent; as his teacher Larry Aaronson says, "he was fearless, hardworking, and very serious about his craft." He would work endlessly at perfecting any character he attempted, from a priest to a Sandinista rebel to Humpty Dumpty (we'd like to see that!) and everything in between. He was always up for any type of play, from comedies to dark, depressing pieces. When he was fifteen, he even spoofed then U. S. President, Ronald Reagan; according to Aaronson, he nailed the president's character dead-on. "Matt *was* Ronald Reagan, even though he looks nothing like him and was just a skinny kid," says Aaronson. "He had Reagan's posture, his voice, he transformed himself into Reagan." And little do people know, but Matt can also sing and dance. Toward the end of his high school career, during an annual program called the Pilot Play, which is a big end-of-the-year drama extravaganza for students in the Pilot Program, Matt entertained his fellow classmates with his own rendition of "Soul Man," complete with Blues Brothers suit and dark shades.

Even though Gerry would allow the occasional solo performance, he focused his students on ensemble plays (plays that include a lot of different characters), in order to help the kids work and develop parts together, as well as giving a chance to perform to as many kids as possible. Matt always stood out among his fellow student actors. Gerry says that even from an early age it was obvious that Matt was going to be a big success. "From the time he was fourteen or fifteen, you could see the incredible presence he had on stage," says Speca. "Even with his squeaky voice, he never wasted a move on stage. He knew even then what it took to be a good actor."

It was at this point that Matt started thinking more seriously about his future career. In addition to getting hired as an extra for any and every film they could find being shot in Boston, Matt and Ben began "taking meetings" with each other in the school cafeteria to talk shop about their futures. Matt looked to Ben for guidance, because even though Ben was younger, he was more experienced in the business of acting, having already clocked many hours as a professional TV actor.

It was probably during this period of meetings that Matt decided it was time to take his acting career to another level. At sixteen, he told his parents he was ready to go pro and decided to take whatever steps necessary. Ben knew a way to help him. Do what they do in Hollywood: get an agent. Ben called up his own agent in New York to set up an audition for Matt.

Matt's parents weren't too thrilled about his decision (surprise, surprise), but they said that he could go to New York City as long as he paid for the trip with his own money. Matt used the two hundred dollars that he had earned doing a T. J. Maxx commercial to get there. The agent thought he had promise and signed him. Ultimately, though, the agent didn't do a whole lot for Matt. But positive thinker that he is, Matt said that perhaps not getting work during this period was for the best, because this way he was able to concentrate on school. His parents would probably agree.

But Matt did land his first role in a major film while he was still in high school. His film debut, *Mystic Pizza* (1988), was actually the movie that jump-started Julia Roberts' career and put Lili Taylor on the movie map. He was seventeen years old at the time and looked even younger. The baby-faced Matt can be seen playing Steamer, the brother of Roberts' rich boyfriend. The only time you see him in the film is during a dinner scene, in which his one line reveals his apprehension about eating "the green stuff" from a lobster.

THE HARVARD YEARS

Though Matt humbly acts like going to Harvard was no big deal, it is in fact a very big deal. It's next to impossible to get in. You have to have most or all of the following: brains, talent, ambition, work ethic, and personality. Matt got in. He graduated from high school in the spring of 1988 and entered college that fall at Harvard. As well-respected as Harvard is, though, it might not have been Matt's first choice. His dad, Kent, says that when Matt was sixteen he turned down his father's offer of tickets to a Boston Red Sox baseball game. Something was up. It wasn't like Matt, who's a huge sports fan, to turn down an opportunity to see his favorite pitcher, Roger Clemens, play. In fact, something was up. At that time, Matt was studying like crazy, hoping to get into Yale University's acclaimed drama program. In hindsight, the Yale application was meaningless, since he later decided to go to Harvard. And for once, Matt wishes he could have suspended his career ambitions for just one night; he had missed an historic baseball game in which former Red Sox pitcher Roger Clemens set a major league record by striking out twenty batters that night.

Matt entered Harvard as an English major, possibly as something to fall back on in case acting didn't pan out. But he was never far from his dream; he wrote on his application essay to Harvard that acting was his first and foremost love. According to Matt, the first line of the essay read: "For as long as I remember, I've wanted to be an actor." It didn't take long for that truth to surface. It was at Harvard that he studied with acting teacher and director David Wheeler. He also took a writing class with former professor Anthony Kubiak. It was in his class where *Good Will Hunting* got its start—originally as a one-act play.

Matt began to take on more than he could handle. In addition to performing in Harvard plays, taking scriptwriting classes, and pursuing his English degree, he also somehow managed to squeeze in performing with a few Boston-based theater groups. One of these was a 1992 Nora

Theater Company production of *Speed of Darkness*, in which he played a tie-dyed T-shirt-wearing teen. At the same time, he was going out on many auditions and starting to get offers for parts in films and made-for-TV movies. Besides being an important experience, one of the big differences about these new roles was that they paid money.

Harvard is hard enough for people who are devoting *all* their time to their schoolwork, let alone for someone also doing auditions, spending whole days (or weeks) on shoots, and memorizing characters' lines. As his time for school work decreased, Matt's temporary solution was to cut back on the number of local projects he was doing so that he could focus on these new film roles. The decision wasn't as easy as one might think. As he told Harry Knowles of the Ain't It Cool News Web site: "I would have done that [more plays] if I could guarantee that I would stay a whole semester. But a lot of times I wasn't, so they'd say, 'Well, this show is going up in a month,' and if I knew I wasn't leaving that month, I'd do it." He does wish that he'd had the time, though, because, as he put it "college theater is fun—doing student-directed stuff is great because everyone gets in there together."

During Matt's sophomore year at Harvard, he was cast as Charlie Robinson in the TNT (cable television) original movie *Rising Son* (1990). He played the troubled son of veteran actors Piper Laurie, (Paul Newman's girlfriend in the classic film *The Hustler*) and Brian Dennehy, who plays Gus

Robinson, a foreman in a Detroit auto factory. In this film, Gus has well-mapped-out plans for how his children can make more of their lives than he has of his own. The only problem is, he hasn't consulted Charlie as to his own wishes. The plot thickens when Charlie, a first-year college student, comes home on break and has to figure out a way to tell his proud and intimidating father that he's dropping out of the pre-med program and possibly leaving school entirely to work on the line with his dad.

Even though *Rising Son* was just a made-for-TV movie, it represented an important milestone in Matt's reception as a serious actor. To begin with, it was one of the first roles where Matt was cast as someone playing his own age rather than as just another cute teenager. "This is not a typical thing for me because I was playing my age. Usually I'm playing a 16- or 17-year-old kid because I have such a baby face," Matt said. The film was also one of the first to get Matt some national attention in the form of glowing praise. Even *The New York Times* made mention of his performance, saying that "it was right on target." And Jack Thomas of the *Boston Globe* wins the award for Matt's future-fame prediction by saying, in 1990, "Remember the name Matt Damon. If he doesn't become a movie star, my name is Robert Redford." In case you've been asleep for the last couple of years, Jack Thomas is still Jack Thomas.

Matt left Harvard again during his junior year when he landed another Charlie role, this time as

Charlie Dillon, a preppy racist in *School Ties* (1992). The movie, set in the 1950s, tells the story of a group of rich kids attending a prestigious prep school. It focuses on their racist attitudes toward their new Jewish quarterback, played by Brendan Fraser. Matt's role was hard won—he went in to read for it more than a dozen times—but it payed off by introducing him to a group of influential, up-and-coming "frat-packers." This group includes Matthew McConaughey, Joaquin Phoenix (River's younger brother), Brendan Fraser, Chris O'Donnell (who nabbed a huge role in *Scent of a Woman*, which both Fraser and Damon auditioned for), Ben Affleck, and Amy Locane *(Melrose Place)*.

In early 1992, Matt auditioned for a part in a modern Western about the famous Apache Indian leader, Geronimo. He got the part. He wasn't the lead and the movie would go on to only moderate success. But for Matt, winning this part represented a graduation of sorts from a particular period in his life: college. His talent was once again dictating his future.

3

MATT'S "REEL" WORLD

In the spring of 1992, things started to get very exciting for Matt—not to mention pretty complicated. He got the part in *Geronimo,* dropped out of Harvard (not something a person does casually), and moved to Los Angeles, mainly so he wouldn't have to keep coast-jumping every other week to audition for parts. On top of all this was the fact that Matt's night job as a screenwriter, soon to be his main focus, was also heating up. Besides, Ben was already living on the West Coast and the two had reason to believe that the script of *Good Will Hunting* might actually have real potential (more about that later). But time-consuming as all this sounds, Matt was at heart still living the college life. According to Ben's brother Casey, "basically, Matt sat around, ate Cheerios, played video games, and scribbled in his notebook." Okay, multi-talented and chock full of ambition? Yes. Mature adult? Not quite yet.

Back up a minute, he dropped out of Harvard? Matt explains it like this to Harry Knowles from the Ain't It Cool News Web site: "What was happening is that I would keep coming back, and I would almost get done with the semester and then I would be yanked out. But I thought it was serving me well, and everyone one at that point was saying *Geronimo* was going to be a big hit, so . . . [laughs]." To this day, Matt still needs about twelve credits to graduate (about two semesters), but that didn't stop him from sporting the traditional cap and gown anyway, and acting like he was part of the graduating class of 1992.

On his way from Cambridge to Los Angeles, Matt stopped off in the wild western plains of central Utah to make *Geronimo: An American Legend* (1993), a film about the defiant Apache Indian leader. He played Lieutenant Britton Davis, a young West Point (the U. S. Army's prestigious military college) graduate who narrates the story, alongside Robert Duvall (one of Matt's acting heroes and star of the recently released film *The Apostle*), Gene Hackman, Wes Studi, and Jason Patric. Prior to filming, the cast was required to take lessons in gun handling and horseback riding. Matt's horse, known as "101" was a seasoned professional; it had been Nicole Kidman's ride in *Far and Away*. The film was a modest success and Matt's performance was generally praised by the critics.

Turning down major movie roles isn't normally something you do when you're crashing on a friend's couch and trying to build a career in Hollywood, unless you're pretty sure you're going to get something better. But that's exactly what Matt did. He must have been riding a pretty big wave of confidence about this time. According to a recent interview, just after *Geronimo* Matt was offered a part in *The Quick and the Dead,* a Western that starred Sharon Stone and Gene Hackman. An impressive offer for any actor. But Matt wasn't impressed. Mainly, he just didn't like the script so he declined the part. He explained it to his surprised agent this way: "You know what I did last night? I watched *Bullitt* [a 1968 police drama featuring Steve McQueen]," he told *Time*. "Robert Duvall drives a cab in that movie, and he has, like, four lines, but he was totally believable, and he was really good, and at the end of the day he was in *Bullitt*. He's in all these great movies because he doesn't do this kind of thing [like *The Quick*]." The part was snapped up by a kid named Leonardo DiCaprio.

Another reason Matt might have been so self-assured was the fact that his other career, as a screenwriter, was starting to look very promising. On November 13, 1994, he and Ben sold an early version of their *Good Will Hunting* script with themselves attached as the lead roles. (More details about this crazy scene can be found in Chapter 4.) Given the fact that *Hunting* would be the perfect vehicle to launch Matt's career (since he wrote the part for himself), he wanted to focus on the screenplay with Ben and make that project happen. After *The Quick and the Dead* offer, whether he intended to or not, Matt started taking on more minor roles that wouldn't demand so much of his time. It had the desired effect of allowing him to focus more of his time on the writing of his own script.

He had a small part in *The Good Old Boys* (1995), another TNT venture starring Academy Award winner Tommy Lee Jones (*The Fugitive, Men in Black*), who also made his debut as a director on this project. Matt played Cotton Calloway, son of Jones' character Hewey Calloway. Matt also had a cameo as Edgar Pudwhacker in *Glory Daze* (1996), which actually starred buddy Ben Affleck as a college student dealing with, of all things, graduating and having to face the real world of life after college. Matt was briefly on screen in *Chasing Amy* (1997), a film by Kevin Smith, who also wrote *Clerks* and *Mallrats*. His role was officially titled "Executive No. 2." Then came the first of a couple of big-time parts.

Courage Under Fire

Even though reviews had been good for Matt in his previous roles, it wasn't until he portrayed a Gulf War soldier in 1996's *Courage Under Fire* that Hollywood insiders really started to take notice. In what would become his breakout film, *Courage* featured him as Ilario, a heroin-addicted marine racked with guilt over the loss of his medical-evacuation pilot captain (Meg Ryan) when they were stuck behind enemy lines in Iraq. He played opposite Denzel Washington, Ryan, and Lou Diamond Phillips. It was during and after *Courage* that big-name directors and actors were starting to respond to Matt's talent. "On his first day of shooting a scene with Denzel [Washington], Denzel and I looked at each other and we both knew what was registering with us—this is the real deal," said Ed Zwick, who directed Matt in *Courage*. "There have been moments when you meet someone for the first time and their talent is immediate. When Matt walked in, it was so abundantly clear that he had the abilities."

Those abilities, as well as his commitment to the role propelled him to lose forty pounds in one-hundred days (for only two days of shooting, mind you) to show the effects that war, drugs, and guilt could have on a person. Because he couldn't afford a nutritionist (and he wasn't a big enough star yet to warrant one), he decided to shed the pounds on his own. His self-prescribed regimen included jogging twelve miles a day (six in the morning, six at night) and eating only plain chicken, egg whites, steamed veggies, and maybe one or two potatoes a day. He also drank pots and pots of coffee each day to give himself energy. He says that this program caused him many fainting spells and made him generally tired all the time. He got down to less than two percent body fat (a percentage usually unheard of except in Olympians and professional athletes) and was a borderline anorexic.

Though the effect of his transformation only added credibility to his overall performance and labeled him as a serious actor, the trauma he inflicted on his body would haunt him for many years afterward. He was lucky that he didn't take it much further. When he finally went to see a doctor after filming, he told Matt that the good news was that his heart didn't shrink (a very serious condition); the bad news was he would have to be on medication for several years to correct the incredible stress he put on his adrenal gland. (This gland maintains a person's metabolism, and problems with it can manifest themselves in weakness, weight loss, nausea, and/or lethargy.) Though Matt would be hard-pressed to go through torturing his body again for a role (or at least if he has to, he can now afford professional help), he has no regrets and considers it simply a business decision.

The Rainmaker

Ultimately, the sacrifice did not go unnoticed, even though Matt claims his phone did not ring for six months afterward. But when it did, it was none other than Oscar-award-winning director Francis Ford Coppola, who had been blown away by the emaciated Ilario and thought his freshness would be perfect for the lead in *The Rainmaker*. Coppola cast him over Edward Norton (who had actually beat out Matt previously for the *Primal Fear* role, which earned Norton an Academy Award nomination) in what was to be Matt's first starring role and his ninth movie. In this 1997 film, based on the bestseller by John Grisham, Matt played attorney Rudy Baylor, the green, over-eager counselor who tries to bring down an evil insurance company. He worked alongside Jon Voight, Danny DeVito, and Claire Danes, whom he dated briefly during filming.

To get a feel for Rudy, Matt went down to Knoxville, Tennessee, and hung out with the locals there— he went to some high school football games, and even tended bar to get a feel for his Southern character. For the shooting of a tense deposition scene, Matt put rocks under his suit to help his character appear as uncomfortable and awkward as possible. It wasn't all serious though. Matt said that Coppola, who loves spontaneity, would play practical jokes on his cast. For instance Coppola enjoyed watching his cast do double takes when they would open a door and find the wrong character standing there. It was even reported in the *Enquirer* that Matt joined in on the pranks and shocked Jon Voight by baring his, uh, "soul" to him during a trial scene. As Matt put it, "You should have seen the look on his face."

All joking aside, *The Rainmaker* was an incredibly important film for Matt's career. He was the star of a major motion picture. The most important critics were becoming aware of his talents. Janet Maslin of *The New York Times* said, "The filmmaker and the cast apparently put a great deal of effort into developing individual performances, and the result is a rich, lifelike texture for the whole film. Damon provides much of this, giving Rudy a quiet authority and courtliness that make him a fine foil to the story's more exuberant figures. . . . Damon is fresh and pensive here in ways that reinvent the character." Most importantly, Matt was finally landing the starring roles and at the same time keeping his perspective on the big picture—a quality without which many young rising stars crash. With his early successes, he didn't let it go to his head, didn't rest on his laurels, or his looks for that matter, and realized that the only way to get better was to keep learning, growing, and improving his craft. "I kind of look at it [acting] as a trade—the only way to get better was to apprentice yourself to the masters," he told Harry Knowles. "I think the masters of today are in films—people like [Robert] Duvall, Denzel Washington, Mickey Rourke, Jon Voight, Francis McDormand, Terry Kinney, Sam Shepard, Minnie, Robin, Stellan Skarsgård—and I . . . get to watch them. I feel like I grow exponentially when I watch them."

It's that kind of commitment to his work that makes him such a standout, and was also what would soon put him on almost all of the major Hollywood directors' wish lists. He describes his goal as similar to that of Robert Redford's character in *The Natural*, who said that when he walks down the street, he wants people to say, "There goes the best." To help him achieve such lofty aspirations, he has been given good advice early in his career by his hero Robert Duvall, whom he met in 1992 while on the set of *Geronimo*. "I followed him [Duvall] around. He taught me immersion [acting method]. He always said, 'Soak it up, soak it up.'" No matter who Matt portrays, he takes his time to understand and respect his character and to learn the character's odd quirks. This is a pretty difficult task, as Matt says, "Learning how to act is like going to another country and trying to learn another language."

He's becoming pretty fluent in that language, and it's paying off on a more personal level. "I'm always pleased with my performances because I know that I couldn't do it any better," he told one interviewer. "I always try my hardest, give it all I've got. If people don't like it, then they don't like it, that's totally up to them. But, I'll never have a regret about it. Just do whatever it takes to get to the truth of the character. I don't think there's any length that you should not go to do that. That's what we do for a living."

Not only is Matt committed to learning from his elders and colleagues, but he truly respects the profession and is very generous with his talents. "I can tell you that he's marvelous to work with," said Teresa Wright, who starred with Matt in *The Rainmaker* and who won an Oscar in 1942 for Best Supporting Actress in *Mrs. Miniver*. "And he's a great help to other actors. He doesn't have a thought about being a picture star. He's interested in being an actor, because he truly loves acting. What makes you interested in the character [Rudy] of that lawyer is that his desire to do a good job is a direct reflection of Matt, who has great sincerity behind what he does and tremendous energy."

The *Rainmaker* role was the final nod that Miramax co-head Harvey Weinstein needed to take the plunge and put Matt and Ben's *Good Will Hunting* script into production, the movie that would make Matt Hollywood's "Next Big Thing."

4

A LITTLE GOOD WILL

THE GREAT PAPER CHASE

"Where there's a will, there's a way," could be the mantra for Matt Damon and Ben Affleck's screenplay *Good Will Hunting*. What started out as a way to create decent roles for themselves, turned into a multimillion-dollar success. It not only shattered the studio box office record, but also made them household names, plastered their faces on magazine covers, gave them A-list actor status (read: big bucks), and won them and their costars countless awards, including a couple of Oscars. Who could have predicted that what started out as a college writing assignment (that was rumored to have gotten a "B"!) could turn into all that?

The genesis of *Good Will Hunting* began on the Harvard University campus. Matt originally wrote it as a one-act for a playwriting class. After the class ended, Matt had about forty pages and no foreseeable ending. With encouragement from his teacher,

Anthony Kubiak, to keep at it and turn it into a feature-length piece, Matt, then twenty-two, turned to his best friend, Ben Affleck, for help. The two started thinking up ways to flesh it out and make it better. In addition to improvising possible scenes together (they are actors after all), they also work-shopped the script (read it aloud with other actors to get feedback on the dialogue) at acting classes at the American Repertory Theater in Boston with director David Wheeler. Then, in 1993, while living in L.A., the two actors decided to really go for it and create their dream roles.

The initial incarnation of the then fifteen-hundred-page script (which would make a ten-hours-plus film) was far more action-adventure oriented than it was a character-driven drama. It depicted the lead character, Will Hunting, as a brainiac who was hired by the FBI to tap into (hack the computer code) and disarm terrorist weapons of mass destruction. Matt and Ben asked their agent to take a look at the script and possibly shop it around, even though they anticipated having to make the film independently. Like most scripts, it met with a lot of deaf ears and they were told "I'll get back to you" many times when they first started putting feelers out for buyers. Some studios expressed interest in the script but not necessarily in Matt and Ben as stars in the film. Talking about these early stages of trying to stir up interest in the script, Matt told the *Boston Globe*, "It was really hard. I'm not going to candy-coat it. It was really depressing and frustrating." They didn't have to wait long, though, for the merit of the script to sell itself.

Some people have called Hollywood the ultimate popularity contest: once something gets a buzz about it, generates a little momentum, everyone wants to get their hands on it. That's exactly what happened with the script of *Good Will Hunting*. Through what Ben calls "smoke and mirrors," the script started to generate heat, and soon the boys found themselves in the middle of a four-day bidding war with most of the major studios. It would have been impossible for them to predict this incredible outcome. Up until this moment it was still a dream, and Matt and Ben were still boys "taking meetings." They were faking it, acting like they knew what they were doing. Ben called themselves the Milli Vanilli (infamous, Grammy-winning lip-syncers) of screenwriters. Then came their initiation into the big leagues. They described the bidding war to John Brodie in *Premiere* magazine like this, " 'When the phone started ringing, we were ready to take the first offer, which was $15,000," Affleck says. "After each call," Damon says, "we were yelling at our agent, Patrick Whitesell, 'Take it! Just take the offer!' "

It was a good thing they didn't jump so soon. When the dust had settled, Castle Rock Entertainment emerged as the victorious studio, purchasing the then action-adventure script (as well as the rights to Matt and Ben's next script), in November 1994, for over half a million dollars, way more money than either of them had ever seen up until that point. In a bit of an understatement, Matt said, "We went from eating Ramen [cheap instant noodle soup] to eating real spaghetti."

SIGN ON THE DOTTED LINE

The sale of the *Hunting* script also marked one of the biggest-ever paydays for a pair of first-time screenwriters. It was actually less money than what they could have gotten for it because offers of one to two million dollars were waved under their noses. But they balked at higher-priced offers because they would have been forced to take a back seat and let their tailor-made characters go to bigger-name actors like Brad Pitt or Leonardo DiCaprio. But, just as Sylvester Stallone did about twenty years earlier with his script *Rocky,* which he wrote, starred in, and which even won the 1976 Oscar for Best Picture, the boys held out for what movie-industry people call a "pay and play" deal. They attached themselves, as Ben said, "like leeches" to the script as not only the film's writers, but also as its stars. They were determined not to sell out. It was a risky move.

For the next year, Matt and Ben, while juggling their other careers as actors, dedicated themselves to reworking the script at Castle Rock's insistence. But it was actually at the suggestion of Liz Glotzer, president of production at Castle Rock, and Rob Reiner, director of the cult classic "mockumentary" *This Is Spinal Tap* and a Castle Rock partner, that the writing duo forget about their original action-adventure plotline and flesh out a story focusing on the characters' relationships. Though in hindsight the suggestion was clearly right on the money, it had the practical outcome of putting Matt and Ben back at square one. As *Hunting* coproducer Chris Moore told *Entertainment Weekly,* "It was a scary moment. We started [all over again] with 63 pages and made it a character story."

As any professional writer will tell you, changing focus like that midway through a script can be even harder than starting from scratch. With everything else they had going on in their careers, it would have been pretty easy to think up excuses to put the film on the back burner for a while just to try to catch their breaths. It wasn't going to happen that way. As Matt told the *Boston Globe,* "we always felt that we would tough it out no matter what, and I think in terms of perseverance we're both really driven. Being a team really helped because when one was down, the other somehow managed to be up. There was never a time when we were both totally deflated."

So instead of giving in, they started just brainstorming—throwing out random ideas to see if anything interesting popped up. As Ben told *Entertainment Weekly,* he and Matt looked at every possible angle for the characters, because "nothing seemed too bad to pursue." In one draft, "Will's therapist, Sean, became Will's construction foreman," in another, "Will and Sean bonded when Will tagged along to Sean's book club meeting." At one point, they even considered one of director Gus Van Sant's wilder ideas, that Ben's character,

Chuckie, Will's best friend in the film, would die at a construction site after a steel beam "squishes him like a bug." Any of these ideas would have made for some pretty strange, or at least pretty different, outcomes for the story line of the film.

Luckily, some other good ideas did surface. A lot of them happened during cross-country road trips. As Matt told Gus Van Sant upon one of their first meetings at a Denny's in L.A., "We [Ben and Matt] tell each other stories while in a particular character, usually to crack each other up or to make sure that Ben doesn't fall asleep at the wheel. When we get into an improv that we both like . . . and dialogue we are relatively excited about, I will open up the glove compartment where I keep my notebook and write down a few notes that we will use later to recall the entire improvisation."

The pair also did a lot of faxing back and forth when they weren't in the same city; they were each other's best audience—trying to make each other laugh or cry. After cooking up hundreds of possible scenes and thousands of lines of dialogue that turned into ten full-script rewrites (always with Ben being the typist and Matt standing in the middle of the room gesturing wildly with his hands), they emerged with what essentially became the version of *Good Will Hunting* that is currently lighting up movie screens around the world.

When Matt and Ben returned to Castle Rock, in October 1995, with their new script, they quickly learned the true meaning of "creative differences."

First they found out that instead of shopping the script around to established directors, the studio had already designated one of its partners, Andrew Scheinman, to direct the film. (Scheinman's only directorial experience was the forgettable *Little Big League*.) Then they learned that Castle Rock intended to shoot the whole film in Toronto, rather than in Boston, to cut production costs. Worst of all, they started to get a sneaking suspicion that no one was actually reading their rewrites. As a joke, they started adding crude and nonsensical lines and scenes to the script; no one ever said a word. Things weren't looking good.

Their worst fears were confirmed when Castle Rock put the script up for sale. Previously interested studios said "no" this time around, mainly because Castle Rock set the price tag at one million dollars. When a script goes up for sale, it often means it's dead in the water. The boys had only thirty days for someone else to buy it, or else Castle Rock would have kept the script and the two would be on the set sidelines watching other guys playing their parts, if it got made at all. In a stroke of good fortune, Ben gave the script to friend and indie director Kevin Smith, who loved it and sent it over to Miramax co-head Harvey Weinstein. Though Miramax initially had passed on the script, Weinstein loved the new version and immediately shelled out the one mil.

Miramax and *Good Will Hunting* were a perfect fit. Miramax is the "indie" (independent) offshoot of Disney. It is run by two brothers, Bob and

Harvey Weinstein. (The company is even named after their mom and dad, Miriam and Max.) During the last few years, they've been riding—maybe even single-handedly creating—the whole indie craze. The kinds of movies they make or buy tend to be thought of as smarter, hipper, and more original. They're also known for being riskier, less formulaic (they don't follow a predictable plot) and less "Hollywood." Hits like *Pulp Fiction, The English Patient,* and *Fargo* are just a few of their huge successes. In fact, in 1997, Miramax produced four out of the five movies nominated for Best Picture and won the big prize for *The English Patient. Good Will Hunting* is just the kind of script that the Brothers Weinstein would jump at. And jump they did.

After Harvey read the script, he contacted Lawrence Bender, the producer of *Pulp Fiction,* to see if he would have any interest in making *Good Will Hunting.* In an interview with *Now Playing,* Bender spoke about the beginnings of the project: "We were at the New York Film Critics Awards in January of '96 and we were snowed in. And Harvey says, 'You know, I got this great script, *Good Will Hunting,* my favorite script at Miramax. I haven't told anyone about it yet and I want to bring you in [to make this movie].' So I read it and it was great. I hadn't met the guys [Matt and Ben] yet but there was something about it. . . . [The script] was very moving. There was a passion. It really hit me at my heart. I met with the guys [Matt and Ben] and they were really cool. They were these young, passionate, obviously very talented guys who were really into it." Things were starting to look up again.

PUTTING IT ALL TOGETHER

Good news comes in waves. The next thing to happen was Miramax giving the okay on their choice for director: Gus Van Sant. According to Matt, Van Sant's official reaction to Matt on the phone was, in his typical laid-back style, "Yeah, I want to direct it. That's if you want to do it. Okay. Bye." Even though there was concern about Van Sant's ability to tell a sentimental story without making it too dark, choosing him to direct the picture turned out to be a terrific move. While Van Sant's best-known films *Drugstore Cowboy* and *My Own Private Idaho* displayed his understanding of the shady worlds of crime and drugs, they were also vivid proof of the director's ability to show off the talents of young actors. His experience directing actors such as Matt Dillon, River Phoenix, and Keanu Reeves in subtle and complex roles (including characters who were orphans) was exactly what a movie like *Good Will Hunting* needed.

But the hiring of Van Sant was by no means decided from the beginning. Another early choice had been Mel Gibson, whose previous big directing success was the 1996 Oscar-winning, *Braveheart* (Gibson won Best Director for the film). The reason for wanting Gibson was his experience in directing a megahit. Though Van Sant had received great critical success for his earlier work, he had never directed something on the scale of *Braveheart*. In the end, the mutual respect between Van Sant and Matt and Ben payed off in the form of a great movie built on subtle yet powerful performances. In regard to the incredible luck of getting Van Sant to direct their film, Ben said in *Interview,* " 'fortune was in favor of us fools'—and we're happy."

They were even happier once Robin Williams said yes to portraying Sean Maguire, Will's therapist. Not only would Robin add his incredible talent to the movie, his big name would also help draw a much larger audience to the theater. (Plus, what actor wouldn't kill for the opportunity to work with someone as funny and talented as Robin?) Rumor has it that Williams could tell early on that he was involved with a sure thing; instead of taking a huge salary for his appearance, he decided to take only a small amount of cash up front and take "points"—a percentage of the box-office proceeds. In other words, he was gambling that the movie would be a huge hit. Sources say that he got as much as ten to fifteen percent of the movie's total gross. If the movie makes its projected three-hundred-million dollars, and Williams gets even ten percent of that . . . well, you can do the math. Good move, Robin.

The part of Skylar, Will's girlfriend in the movie, was given to the first actress who read for the part, Minnie Driver. During the audition, in which she read with Matt, she made the guys in the room cry (Matt, Ben, Van Sant, coproducer Chris Moore, and producer Lawrence Bender). Even though they auditioned more women, they knew they were just going through the motions—Minnie was just too perfect to even consider anyone else. The role of Gerry Lambeau, the professor who takes Will under his wing, was more difficult to cast, but it finally went to *Breaking the Waves* star Stellan Skarsgård, a Swedish actor (with just the right accent for an MIT math prof) who's just starting to make a name for himself on this side of the Atlantic.

Rounding out the cast were Will and Chuckie's buddies Morgan and Billy, played by Casey Affleck (Ben's brother) and Cole Hauser, respectively. George Plimpton parodies himself as the stodgy, old-school psychologist who just can't deal with a stubborn, young genius like Will. (For those old enough to remember, George Plimpton was the goofy commercial spokesman for an early failed video game system known as Intellivision.)

ON THE SET

The crew spent four weeks shooting in Boston. Many of the outdoor shots are of MIT. To save on production costs, most of the indoor scenes were shot in Toronto. (Toronto is becoming known as "Canada's Hollywood" because so many films and TV shows are now being shot there. They have many of the same production capabilities as they do in L.A., but it's way cheaper.) The indoor exceptions were the scenes at South Boston's

L Street Tavern and at the Tasty, the burger joint where Skylar and Will have their first date. Since the movie came out, South Boston is experiencing some good effects from the exposure. Tourists are now venturing to the neighborhood to check it out and to see where the film was shot. And MIT students are cheering Matt and Ben for confirming their belief that Harvard students (MIT's rivals) are rich, snooty, and pretentious!

When anyone—cast or crew—talks about the shooting of *Good Will Hunting,* he or she almost always seems to make reference to Gus Van Sant's laid-back directing style and how easy it was for everyone to work with him. That smooth rapport shows through in the final product. Matt told the *Los Angeles Times,* "He has an ability—people would call it 'his eye'—he always puts the camera in an extraordinarily uninhibiting place. And it's always the right place, to pick up these moments of humanity." Matt also credited the D.P. (director of photography), Yves Escoffier, for his ability to create an actor's environment. Whereas most D.P.s set up so many lights (which generate intense heat) that it feels like asphalt in August, Yves builds a totally natural light environment that makes it easy for actors to focus on acting.

THE STORY

In case you've been under a rock since late 1997 and haven't seen *Good Will Hunting,* here's a quick rundown on its basic plot points. In a very believable (and somewhat close-to-home) role, Matt plays Will Hunting, a college-age orphan growing up alone in South Boston's poorer neighborhoods. He also just happens to be a genius, especially in math. To make money, he works as a janitor at (by a sweet twist of fate) Massachusetts Institute of Technology (MIT), one of the world's most prestigious science universities. Will advertises the precocious powers of his brain by solving next-to-impossible equations that an MIT math professor, Gerry Lambeau (Stellan Skarsgård), leaves on the hallway chalkboard for any of his daring students to attempt.

Gerry is dumbfounded when he discovers that someone is able to solve his equations, overnight no less. He's even more blown away when he finds out that credit goes not to one of his students, but instead to a kid from South Boston who's making a living mopping up the halls at night. Sensing his obvious genius, Gerry immediately tries to pull a somewhat-unwilling Will Hunting into the institutional world of academics. But he discovers it's not that easy.

At about the same time, Will and his buddies get into a fight with some local kids and Will ends up hitting a cop, which lands him in the slammer. Gerry wants to help Will, partly for Will's sake, but just as much for his own. But Will's a gruff kid from broken homes, and he's learned never to trust authority. In some pretty funny scenes, Gerry brings in several psychologists—some, pipe-smoking intellectuals, others, just-plain-weird types—to try to help Will function in the foreign and confusing worlds of academia and corporate America. Will's too smart, and smart-aleck, to respect anyone who's had life so easy; he's not about to go soft just because some old stuffed shirt tells him everything's gonna be okay.

Enter Sean McGuire, portrayed by Robin Williams. Sean is an old friend of Gerry's and teaches psychology at a lesser-known community college. He's had a bumpier road than Gerry and you can tell that while there's some mutual respect, there's also a bit of resentment toward his old friend. Gerry, who can't help condescending to his old pal, thinks that Sean can help Will because he too is from Southie. He can relate. Williams plays Sean brilliantly, a vulnerability showing through his wisdom—never before seen in any of Williams' previous characters. He's not the heroic, wise old sage from *The Dead Poets Society* nor is he playing the always-jokey ham he was in *Good Morning, Vietnam*.

About this time, Will meets Skylar, played by Minnie Driver. He's into her from the beginning, but he's got the same problem: can he stay true to his Southie roots and his buddies and still take advantage of the opportunities his photographic memory offers? It's a tough choice but he's got a great supporting cast, especially Ben Affleck, who plays Will's best friend, Chuckie. Matt sums up the film in *Interview,* "It's like a comedy and a drama and a coming-of-age story."

In *Hunting,* Matt outperforms all his previous roles. He nails the character and makes all his relationships completely believable. He'd finally realized his dream, writing himself a tailor-made role and getting it perfectly right.

5

GOOD WILL MAKES GOOD

Five years of rewrites, second-thoughts, misfires. Action movie, drama, comedy, or a little of all? Starting over almost completely from scratch. But, where there's a will . . . In industry jargon, the film was now "in the can." It was shot and edited, film duplicates (what they show in the theaters) were made and distributed to cinemas around the country. At the time, the general media perception was at best a modest anticipation about the film: two untested screenwriters (who are really just cute actors, right?) in another "feel good, against the odds" Robin Williams vehicle. To most it sounded interesting, but was probably at best, just another *Dead Poets Society* inspirational. But after all, Gus Van Sant did direct it, so maybe it's weird enough to not be too sentimental and boring, or its plot too obvious.

Modest anticipation turned into an insider buzz

in New York and Hollywood as advance premieres of the movie showed in a few different venues. There was a special screening in a Harvard Square theater. (In fact, as a bit of playfulness for Matt and Ben, it was the very same theater they'd been kicked out of for sneaking into many times as kids.) There was also a special opening and party in New York City that was part of a charity organization known as the Fresh Air Fund. The film premiered to wider audiences in Los Angeles and New York on December 5, 1997, and came out nationwide right after the new year.

Then the reviews started coming in. Janet Maslin of *The New York Times* had nothing but praise for the movie on all levels. About the screenplay: "Two young actors [Matt and Ben] with soaring reputations have written themselves a smart and touching screenplay, then seen it directed with style, shrewdness and clarity by Gus Van Sant. There couldn't be a better choice than the unsentimental Van Sant for material like this. . . . The script's bare bones are familiar, yet the film also has fine acting, steady momentum, a sharp eye and a very warm heart." On Matt: "It turns out that Will [is] the most likably recalcitrant coming-of-age character this side of Gilbert Grape. . . ." and later in the review, "Damon, very much the supernova, is mercurial in ways that keep his character steadily surprising." On Robin Williams: "the screenplay offers Robin Williams the rare serious role that takes full advantage of his talents." On Gus Van Sant: "Van Sant tacitly dramatizes the class tensions at the heart of

MAXINE DIAMOND

this story. Whether Will sees refuge or honor in a life of bricklaying, the film captures the full extent of his turmoil." On Minnie Driver: "As the teasing, beautiful medical student who can peer into Will's soul as easily as she can tell a dirty joke, Minnie Driver adds further charm to an already wise, inviting story."

Harry Knowles of the Ain't It Cool News Web site was even more impressed: "I want him [Ben] to know that he and his best friend [Matt] made a movie that shook me. That reached out and touched me right down to the fiber of my being. I was blown away." The list of rave reviews could go on for pages. It was almost universally lauded as being one of the year's top five films. All the individual performances were praised, with Matt, Robin, and Minnie taking the lion's share of positive commentary.

Then it was the public's turn to rave. Natalie Pelligrino, twenty-seven, of Santa Barbara, California, saw the movie five times. "I'm embarrassed by how much I like it," she says. "I cry every time." Lynn Smith of the *Los Angeles Times* asked people what they thought about the film. "It had everything. It was sad. It was hilarious," said Nasim Pedrad, sixteen, of Irvine, California. *Hunting* even became her favorite movie of all time, replacing *Titanic*. She also said that Damon was "real" and "down to earth" and also (uh oh) that he was even more attractive than king of hearts Leonardo DiCaprio. A friend of hers, Deedee Nichols, sixteen, agreed with this assessment and added, "This

Matt
Damon

Rising Son (1990)
with Piper Laurie

TNT/Shooting Star

School Ties
(1992)

Paramount
Pictures/Shooting
Star

Armando Gallo/Retna

Geronimo
(1994)

Columbia/Shooting Star

Courage Under Fire (1996) with Meg Ryan

Shooting Star

Matt at the
Courage Under Fire
premiere
Terry Lilly/Shooting Star

*John Grisham's
The Rainmaker*
(1997) Photofest

Matt and Robin Williams in *Good Will Hunting* (1997) Photofest

Matt and Ben Affleck at the Golden Globe Awards   Ron Davis/Shooting Star

Ron Davis/Shooting Star

Matt and Ben
display their
Oscars for Best
Original
Screenplay
AP/Wide World Photos

Matt and
Ed Norton
on the set of
Rounders (1998)
Bill Davila/Retna

shows that Matt Damon is beyond good-looking. He's a good actor." Pretty much everyone liked the film, with most comments ranging from, "It's hard not to like," to "It changed my life." It affected young and old alike; Jim Levine, another Lynn Smith interviewee, stated, "It's definitely a good movie. My father, who's 70, had seen the movie, and he thoroughly enjoyed it."

AWARD THE GOOD

It's fitting that a film that was such a labor of love would reap countless awards. Since the film's release in December 1997, Matt and Ben picked up Best Original Screenplay awards from the Broadcast Film Critics Association, the Florida Film Critics Circle Awards, and the Golden Globes. Other *Hunting* cast and crew were duly honored as well, with acting nods going to Robin Williams and Minnie Driver and directing awards going to Gus Van Sant. Matt and Minnie even won the male and female Stars of Tomorrow awards at the annual ShoWest conference for theater owners held in Las Vegas in March 1998. The award put Matt and Minnie in some pretty good company: Stars of Tomorrow from previous years include Claire Danes, Winona Ryder, Chris O'Donnell and Brad Pitt. (It also put Matt in the almost embarrassing spot of having dated three of the winners of the award. Surely that's a record in itself.)

Of course the sweetest and most gratifying nominations and awards came from the granddaddy of them all, the Academy Awards, from which *Hunting* picked up nine Oscar nominations: Best Picture, Best Director, Best Film Editing, Best Music Score, Best Song, Best Actor (Matt), Best Supporting Actor (Robin Williams), Best Supporting Actress (Minnie), and Best Original Screenplay. When Matt heard the good news on February 10, 1998, he was in Atlantic City filming *Rounders*. The calls he made were in this order: Ben; his mom, Nancy; his dad, Kent; and his brother, Kyle. In addition to being overwhelmed and shell-shocked by the all the nominations, Matt was floored to be forever linked with the other four 1998 nominees: acting legends Jack Nicholson, Robert Duvall, Dustin Hoffman, and Peter Fonda. And for Matt, that was as much of an honor as actually winning.

Prior to the star-studded evening that is the Oscars, Matt and Ben were among the A-list guests (in Hollywood lingo, the most important people on the guest list) along with Madonna, Demi Moore, Ed Norton, and Neve Campbell at Miramax's famous pre-Oscar party, which was held at the Regent Beverly Wilshire Hotel on the night before the Oscars. The highlight of that evening came when Miramax co-head Harvey Weinstein had this year's Oscar nominees give performances of other movie scenes. Ben and Matt cracked up the guests with their rendition of a scene from *The Wings of the Dove*, with Ben playing Helena Bonham Carter's role (donning Madonna's Jean-Paul Gaultier coat) opposite Matt, who played Linus Roache's character. Returning the favor, Carter and fellow Brit Judi Dench (*Mrs. Brown*) took their turn as Will and Chuckie from *Hunting*, re-creating the scene, hard hats and all, where Chuckie makes it clear to Will that he must utilize his God-given talents.

The evening of March 23, 1998, at Los Angeles' Shrine Auditorium, saw Matt and Ben (both wearing Armani tuxes) strolling the red carpet with their moms and waving to the screaming fans. Robin Williams got things started by winning his first-ever Oscar for Best Supporting Actor. Williams' previous nominations included *Good Morning, Vietnam, Dead Poets Society,* and *The Fisher King.* In his acceptance speech, he expressed his appreciation to Matt and Ben and then requested that he see some ID (because to him, they still seem like kids).

Matt and Ben won the movie's second Oscar for Best Original Screenplay. The two bounded up on stage after much hugging from their moms and Williams. After being handed the statuettes by Hollywood's grumpiest old men, Walter Matthau and Jack Lemmon, they proceeded to give this year's "Cuba Gooding, Jr. acceptance-speech moment," one filled with genuine surprise and uncontrolled excitement. The first thing Ben said was "I just said to Matt, 'Losing would suck and winning would be really, really scary.' You know, it's really, really scary." The two proceeded to start shouting out names of people to thank, including Chris Moore, the film's coproducer; Ben's brother, Casey, who's also in the film; and of course their families and friends back home in Boston. They admitted later that the one important person they forgot to thank was Kevin Smith, who originally took the film to Miramax.

It was a good thing that they didn't forget to mention their hometown of Boston, because the patrons of the L Street Tavern, where many *Hunting* scenes were shot, were dressed to the nines in rented tuxes and gowns clinking glasses to celebrate Matt and Ben's Oscar success. The event, which three-hundred people attended, was Southie's (what the locals call South Boston) version of the Academy Awards, and orchestrated by L Street's owner, Jackie Woods. Not only was the bar filled to capacity, but it was complete with an adjacent heated tent and two big-screen TVs, and was even visited by the town's current mayor, its former mayor, and the governor of Massachusetts. And in another area of Boston, a group of MIT students also wanted to show their love to *Good Will Hunting*. The MIT Hacking Society, a group known to pull off outrageous and unexplainable pranks (in 1994, the Hackers managed to somehow hoist a cop car on top of a big building on the MIT campus), wanted to present the film, as well as the people of South Boston, with their third Oscar. Around 8 P.M. on March 24, the lights in MIT's eighteen-story Green Building went on in the pattern of an Oscar statuette.

But with the sweetness of *Hunting*'s success came bitter criticism. Right before the Oscars, rumors started circulating about whether Matt and Ben really were the writers of the script. The stories fell into three categories: First, that Matt and Ben bought the original story from a third party; second, that if the original tale did come from Matt's one-act play and had been performed in that format, the duo would lose their "original screenplay" Oscar nomination; and third, that noted screenwriter William Goldman (who wrote *Butch Cassidy and the Sundance Kid*) was the real author of the script.

A spokesperson from Miramax made a point of shooting down the rumors in *Daily Variety,* saying that Matt and Ben bought only the title from a Harvard classmate; the one-act play was never performed prior to the screening of the film; and Goldman only talked to the pair during one afternoon about their script. To further refute the claims, Ben made a World Wide Web posting on the News Askew Web site last March, saying "Matt and I wrote the script from beginning to end. We sat down with William Goldman for an afternoon and chatted about his current movie [*Forget Paris*]. Here is the simple fact: People are fighting like mad over credit for various screenplays [*Amistad, Wag the Dog*], why wouldn't they come forward and arbitrate? I have the handwritten various drafts from beginning to end at home. We wrote it. That's all. But I take it as a backhanded compliment that people are so incredulous."

But regardless of a few sour grapes, Matt and Ben came off as big winners, not only for their film, but for their futures as well. It is being predicted that because of the Oscar success, *Good Will Hunting* will make as much as three-hundred-million dollars worldwide. It is also being said that Matt's asking price for acting could jump from his current reported three-hundred-thousand-dollar price tag, to a possible five-million dollars. Miramax's Harvey and Bob Weinstein can pat themselves on the back for spending their money wisely: it cost about ten-million dollars to make the film, and now *Hunting* has set the in-house record for Miramax's highest-grossing film of all time. And it has a lot more life left, with the film being released overseas in February 1998 and the video version set to come out in July 1998. The film has also beat out Miramax's other high box office winner *Pulp Fiction* by surpassing the one-hundred-twenty-million dollar mark; and it's still raking it in.

Not bad for a couple of guys just driving around trying to make each other laugh.

6

THE NEXT BIG THING

Now he's a star, all the rage, the next big thing. A huge box office success, his picture is all over television, magazines, and Web sites, he's got an Oscar(!), and he's still in his twenties. His phone is ringing off the hook. And not without good reason: as an actor and a writer, Matt Damon is one of those rare people who couple a pure ability with a real respect for and dedication to his craft. Not to mention those gorgeous blue eyes and cute smile— that phone will be ringing for years to come.

Even before *The Rainmaker* or *Good Will Hunting* were out in theaters, Steven Spielberg had already tapped into Matt's talent for the title role in his upcoming *Saving Private Ryan* (opposite Tom Hanks). The movie wrapped filming in fall 1997 in England. In it he plays a World War II soldier who's stuck behind enemy lines. Matt met Spielberg, a friend of Robin Williams, while on the set of *Good*

Will Hunting; Spielberg was shooting *Amistad* at the same time in the Boston Commons area. Williams took Matt over to the *Amistad* set, and Spielberg didn't recognize Matt as the emaciated heroin-addict soldier in *Courage Under Fire.* Upon seeing Matt, Spielberg thought he looked familiar but couldn't place him. Matt recounted this first Spielberg meeting on *The Oprah Winfrey Show:* "He said, 'Do I know you? Are you the guy from . . .' and I said, 'Yeah.' He said, 'Did you gain some weight?'" Impressed with his commitment to the Ilario character, Spielberg chose Matt to play the role of Private Ryan. *Courage Under Fire* had come through for him again. The Spielberg film is scheduled to be out mid-July 1998.

In December 1997, Matt started filming *Rounders,* his next starring role for which he is reportedly getting six-hundred-thousand dollars, much less than his post-Oscar asking price. *Rounders* represents his entry into the world of choosing the parts he will play, rather than just taking whatever he can get. He can now afford to be picky, and the scripts handed to him these days aren't from other actors' reject piles (well, except maybe from Tom Cruise's). As he humbly told *Vanity Fair* in the December 1997 issue, in which he was featured on the cover, "I can't believe I'm in a position where I have to turn down work. This has never happened." The film, which is directed by *The Last Seduction's* John Dahl, is the tale of New York's underground poker players. Matt stars alongside Edward Norton (*The People vs. Larry Flynt*), who plays a freshly sprung ex-con who needs fast cash and enlists his law-school buddy and recovering compulsive gambler (Matt) to help him pay off loan-shark debts.

To help the boys exchange their nice-guy grins for serious poker faces, Matt and Edward started frequenting New York's private underground poker clubs and casinos to learn firsthand the tools of the trade. The results are paying off: they've started winning a few *real* high-stakes games. They even took Miramax co-heads, Harvey and Bob Weinstein, for about twelve hundred dollars during one late-night session, but given the box-office performance of *Hunting,* they're probably not too worried about losing a thousand bucks to Matt and his new pal, Ed. *Rounders* was filmed almost entirely in New York and also features veteran actors Martin Landau, John Turturro, and John Malkovich.

In March 1998, after filming wrapped with *Rounders* and after the Oscars, Matt headed to Pittsburgh with Ben Affleck to start shooting Kevin Smith's next venture, *Dogma,* whose working title is *Bearclaw.* In this comedy about Catholicism, Matt and Ben once again play best buddies who are kicked out of heaven to live in Wisconsin forever. Matt and Ben portray fallen angels Loki and Bartelby. The two try to figure out how to get back into heaven and God's good graces.

It's been rumored that Matt and Ben asked Kevin to include a scene that would poke fun at Robin Williams. To tease Robin for his constant joking about wanting to see their IDs, the boys

wanted to take a dig at one of Robin's goofier on-
screen performances. To do this, Matt and Ben
wrote in some lines for their characters. Bartelby
reportedly asks the demon Azrael (played by Jason
Lee) what hell is like. Azrael responds, "Give you a
hint: They've been playing *Mrs. Doubtfire* continu-
ously for two years now." Loki incredulously reacts
saying, "that is punishment." (*Mrs. Doubtfire* was
the movie where Robin Williams dressed up like an
old housemaid so he could spend time with his
kids.) Joining in on the *Dogma* fun will be several
other notable young stars, including Salma Hayek
(*Fools Rush In*), Linda Fiorentino (*The Last Seduction*), and Chris Rock (*Saturday Night Live*). Look
for the film to be released sometime in late 1998.

Matt's star power has grown in ways other than
just his asking price. In December 1997, he almost
inadvertently pulled the plug on a thirty-five-
million-dollar project when he turned down an offer
to star in *To Live Again,* an epic-length Civil War
film directed by Ang Lee (who directed *Sense and
Sensibility* and *The Ice Storm*). Fox Searchlight, the
studio making the film, dropped the project when
they found out that Damon had opted to work on
another film. (It has since been picked up by
Universal and will star Skeet Ulrich and Jewel.)

He passed on the part so that he could take the
title role in Oscar-winning director Anthony Minghella's *The Talented Mr. Ripley*. Set in the 1950s,
the film is Minghella's (who directed the 1996
Oscar Best Picture, *The English Patient*) adaptation of Patricia Highsmith's mystery novel of the

same name and is essentially a remake of the 1960 film *Purple Noon*. Matt will play a creepily charming psychopath opposite Gwyneth Paltrow, Ben's current girlfriend. This type of character is a new one for Matt and one that he finds "fascinating." As he told Mr. Showbiz online, "It's certainly the most unconventional in terms of movies I've done. As Anthony [Minghella] says, he's going to be accused of making another big art-house movie. The guy [Ripley] goes and falls in love with this man and his life—to the point where he wants to be in his skin."

When asked about the type of research one does to get into the head of a cultured sociopath, Matt said, "I want to be very well-versed in opera and jazz, which are very important to the movie. I want to be fluent in Italian. And I'm going to take an etiquette class. . . . I'm more beer and Ripley is more . . . delicate. . . . I'll lose 20 pounds." Of course, Minghella has already okayed a nutritionist. Matt flies to Italy to start shooting in August 1998.

Though we won't see him, we'll hear Matt as he voices the character of Cale in an animated sci-fi film called *Planet Ice*. The futuristic setting of the movie shows Earth destroyed by an evil alien race. Cale, a nineteen-year-old boy who grew up around the aliens, makes it his mission to save mankind. Matt will team up with Bill Pullman (*Twister*), Drew Barrymore, and Nathan Lane (*The Birdcage*), among others, for this film, which will probably be out sometime in 1999.

Also in 1999, watch for Matt in *Training Day,* in which he'll star with Samuel L. Jackson (*Jackie Brown, Pulp Fiction*). Matt will play a rookie cop, who is partnered with a hardened police vet, on his first day of work with the LAPD undercover narcotics squad.

Matt's costars in *Hunting* are also reaping the benefits of the film's huge success. Robin Williams wrapped production on the fantasy *What Dreams May Come* with Cuba Gooding, Jr., last year's Best Supporting Actor. Williams is also executive producing and playing a war hero in next year's release *Jakob the Liar.* He's also got about fifteen other things happening, including a reprisal of his character Armand Goldman in a currently untitled sequel to *The Birdcage.*

Minnie Driver recently wrapped production on *The Governess* in which she played Rosina Da Silva. She is now costarring with Nigel Hawthorne in a film called *At Shashem Farm.* She's actually coproducing the film with her sister Kate. Minnie also just signed on to a new project called *The Ideal Husband.* In it, she plays a sister-in-law to a unfaithful politician.

Stellan Skarsgård, the Swedish actor who played Gerry, Will Hunting's math mentor, is currently working with Robert DeNiro and Jonathan Pryce in *Ronin*—an epic film about a group of adults embarking on a dangerous political mission at the end of the cold war.

In addition to all of the films he's working on with Matt, Ben Affleck is crazy busy. He's currently filming *200 Cigarettes* in New York with Courtney Love and Christina Ricci. The setting for the film is New York's East Village, New Year's Eve 1981. It tells the stories of many different characters on their way to the same party. Sounds interesting. He's also flying to London to do a film called *Shakespeare in Love,* which appropriately costars his current squeeze Gwyneth Paltrow. Ben's also done shooting *Armageddon,* an action-adventure flick which costars the hero of the *Die Hard* series, Bruce Willis, and will be out in the summer of 1998.

Of course, now that Matt and Ben have proven themselves as writers, the two are trying to find time (good luck!) to work on some of their own future writing and acting projects. Actually, they not only should find time, they are contracted to do so. Miramax has already signed a two-picture deal with them, and Castle Rock Entertainment retained the original rights to their next film-writing project.

They've already started working on their script for Castle Rock. The working title for the film is *Half Way House.* It's a story about a pair of counselors working in a mental institution. The concept is reportedly based on true stories told by a friend of theirs about his experiences working in an institutional environment. At first, both Matt and Ben were going to play counselors, but now Matt wants to portray one of the patients. They've denied the rumors that they are dragging their feet a little bit on finishing this project because their original dealings with Castle Rock on the *Hunting* script went so badly.

Who knows when they found time, but they've also finished a romantic-comedy script called *Like a Rock* for Miramax that they'll start shooting once they wrap up their current projects. Ben will play the romantic lead, just like Matt did in *Hunting*. A lesser-known project they're also working on is called *The Wishbones*. This time they're doing a screenplay adaptation based on the first novel of the same name by Tom Perrotta. The film, which would also star, you guessed it, Matt and Ben, will focus on the ups and downs of a New Jersey rock band that performs cover songs at wedding receptions.

It doesn't look like Matt or Ben will be finishing those degrees anytime soon.

7

MATT'S LOVE LINES

As Matt's ever-rising star continues to shoot up into the stratosphere, his love life will be increasingly in the public eye. Linked with some of Hollywood's most eligible bachelorettes, Matt seems to have it all: good looks, a promising acting career, and no shortage of dates. But finding romance wasn't always so easy for Matt.

Though Matt was popular in high school, his senior prom date wasn't as impressed with him as he was with her. As he told *In Style* magazine, the senior prom turned out to be one of his most memorable bad dates. "My senior prom . . . the girl that I went with hooked up with another guy, while I was in the room—hopelessly in love, crying myself to sleep. I mean I was heartbroken, crestfallen. And that was, without a doubt, the worst date of my life." Though he thought the girl was pretty, he now thinks that there are a lot of other girls he would rather have taken to the prom. (Do you think that girl is kicking herself today?)

Even while in college, Matt's romantic encounters didn't seem to fare any better. While studying English at Harvard, Matt started dating a girl by the name of Skylar Statenstein, a pre-med student. The similarity of this real-life relationship with the on-screen romance between *Good Will Hunting*'s Will and Skylar is not coincidental. Minnie Driver's character, Skylar, was based on his real-life true love, who now works as an emergency room doctor in California. As it turns out, the real-life Skylar did leave Matt to further her medical studies (just like the Skylar in *Hunting*), but she went to New York to attend Columbia University, unlike Minnie's Skylar who went west to study at Stanford. And though Matt has claimed that they tried to keep up a long-distance relationship—she in New York, he in L.A.—the real Skylar, whom he calls his college sweetheart, wound up marrying Lars Ulrich, the drummer for the heavy metal rock band Metallica. This was a move Matt was none too impressed with. As he told *Movieline* magazine, she ended up with "a rock star who's got $80 million and his own jet . . . a bad rock star, too."

Matt's sour grapes, though, didn't seem to slow him down at all. For a short while he was linked with models Bridget Hall and then Kara Sands, whom he was dating at the start of filming of *The Rainmaker* in November 1996. Then, while he was on the set of *The Rainmaker,* he became smitten with his leading lady, eighteen-year-old Claire

Danes, who plays Kelly, the abused young wife of Cliff Riker. Matt's character, Rudy Baylor, falls for Kelly as he tries to help her escape her abusive husband. Matt seemed in awe not only of Claire's beauty, but also of her talent. He expressed his appreciation of her ability to tap into sadness at a moment's notice, "She's so close to her emotions," he said in *Entertainment Weekly*. "I remember we had to do an emotional scene in which Claire had to bawl her eyes out over and over and over again. After the scene was finished . . . she told me she was thinking about this sad story . . . she'd seen on HBO. Most people are too desensitized to have that sort of thing affect them. But Claire looks around, sees sadness in the world, and channels it. That's an amazing skill for a person her age." Even though Matt greatly admired Claire, once the film wrapped, so did the romance. Perhaps this was the start of Matt's serial location dating.

Just like they say, life imitates art. Matt became love struck with yet another big screen costar. This time it was Minnie Driver and it started during the shooting of *Good Will Hunting*. Minnie, a twenty-seven-year-old British actress who gained twenty pounds to play opposite Chris O'Donnell in *Circle of Friends*, met Matt for the first time when she auditioned for the role of Skylar in New York. Once again, Matt was impressed with the acting abilities of his leading lady and even said that during the initial audition with her, he was rendered speechless. "It was intimidating when she walked into the room," said Matt in an interview with Ain't It Cool

News' Harry Knowles. "We started doing this scene in the movie where we get in a huge fight [when Will tells Skylar that he doesn't love her], and she did it three times in three different accents [English, American, Irish]. . . . And finally, she's doing it in this Irish accent and it's the third time she's doing it—she starts the scene and I, like, totally blanked. After four and a half years of trying to get this movie made, I didn't know where I was, who I was, or what was going on. And she's standing there with the Cheshire cat smile thinking, 'Would you like to join me in the scene or are you gonna stand there with your tongue hanging out?'" Apparently, he took her up on both offers.

Matt's relationship with Minnie lasted longer than the one with Claire and even took them to another continent. The two were together in the summer of 1997, prior to the release of *Hunting*, while they each were working on their next projects. Minnie was filming *The Governess* in England and Scotland, and Matt was in the British Isles playing the title character for Steven Spielberg's *Saving Private Ryan*. It was even reported that Minnie spent that following Thanksgiving with Matt's family in Boston.

But it wasn't long after the premiere of *Hunting* in December that Matt announced on *Oprah* that he was single again. Rumor has it that he effectively broke up with her on that show, when he said, "I was with Minnie for a while, but we're not romantically involved anymore. We're just really good friends. I love her dearly." The timing of their breakup really couldn't have been more terrible considering all of the awards shows at which the two would have to both be present, because it's been reported that Minnie was not happy about the breakup. (But, don't feel too bad for Minnie, because since the Oscars, she's been seen hanging out with Elliott Smith, who was nominated for an Oscar for best song for "Miss Misery," a song he wrote for *Good Will Hunting.* She's also been seen out with Taylor Hawkins, the drummer for the band The Foo Fighters.)

Never single for very long, Matt was back on the prowl and was seen hanging out with Winona Ryder at many a party shortly after the *Oprah* interview. The couple has even been seen double dating with Ben and his flame, Gwyneth Paltrow (whose most recent romance, in case you just moved here from Mars, was Brad Pitt; she was even engaged to him for a couple of years). As reported in the *Star,* Gwyneth, who happens to be Winona's best friend, set Matt and Winona up even though Gwyneth and Minnie were supposedly friends, having worked together on *Sleepers.* But even while Matt was dating Winona, rumors were flying around about Matt's attraction to *Ally McBeal's* Calista Flockhart, and that *Titanic's* Kate Winslet slipped Matt her number at the Golden Globes. But Matt and Winona still seem pretty tight. (Perhaps they share stories about growing up in a commune. Winona also spent some of her formative years living on a commune-style ranch with her parents in Northern California.) Wow. Hollywood's even more complicated than high school; maybe it really is the ultimate popularity contest.

8

GETTING HOT,
KEEPING COOL

Hollywood may be knocking on Matt's door offering him instant fame and big star clout, setting him up to be the next "It Boy," but he's not interested in playing that role. On the slim chance that he would be, his family wouldn't hear of it. "My family doesn't let me get away with anything," said Matt in *Daily Variety*. "They bring me back down to earth and make me realize that my fame doesn't absolve me of being a good human being."

But this doesn't keep Matt's mom, Nancy, from worrying about him and the repercussions he faces from a lack of privacy with constant public and media scrutiny. "It's hard to become a public person so fast and feel okay," she told the *Cambridge Chronicle*, ". . . to lose your privacy and have almost nowhere you can go and feel privacy." She's also more than a little concerned about his newfound power to make or break a film depending on whether he says yes to a project, something he already experienced with turning down director Ang Lee's next film. "Suddenly Matthew isn't just a regular person like the rest of us," said Nancy. "He's suddenly someone they treat as glamorous or exciting or more powerful than they are. They . . . get all excited when they are in a room with him, and they let him talk on and on. It has to affect him."

Nancy is not the only one concerned for Matt and his ability to maintain a clear perspective on his recent fame and fortune. His high school teachers have also expressed their apprehension. "It'll be the greatest crime if he turns out to be a jerk," says Gerry Speca, his high school drama teacher. "But he has great respect for his mother and he knows there would be much accounting for his actions when it comes to her." But Speca believes that he can handle it "if he comes back to the notion that this profession is about the work and not the adulation."

Matt's high school history teacher, Larry Aaronson, agrees with Speca and says that there's no need to worry about Matt and Ben because they weren't brought up to seek fame for fame's sake. "It's [Ben and Matt's critical success] great for their careers, but it also has the power to distort reality," said Aaronson in the *Chronicle*. "I mean, how do you live with this kind of fame and remain decent, keep your integrity, and not get exploited by the media? It's really hard. But, I think [Matt and Ben] have been raised too well to let that happen."

Nancy seems to be at the core of Matt's ability to maintain a down-to-earth perspective. When she sees the potential for Matt to let all that attention go to his head, she brings him back down to reality. She seems to have a knack for putting things into perspective for Matt. During the phone call to his mother right after Matt got word that *Good Will Hunting* nabbed nine Oscar nominations, his mom's reaction was not quite what he expected. Though she was happy for her son, she was more interested and surprised that *The Boxer,* starring Daniel Day-Lewis, hadn't received a single nod. "When I told her *The Boxer* didn't get nominated for anything she said, 'How can one movie get nine nominations, and a totally profound film like that get none?'" Matt told the *Boston Globe.* "And I said, 'But, Ma, it was my movie!' and she said, 'I know, sweetie, but it just really makes me mad.'"

It doesn't look like Matt's mom has to worry, though, because he works hard at his craft and does so while respecting his colleagues. His down-to-earth quality has even been noticed and appreciated by his cast and crew. As Harvey Weinstein put it, "He is exceptionally bright, honest, and level-headed and has both his feet planted firmly on the ground, which is a hard thing to do in this business."

Brian Dennehy, who starred with Matt in *Rising Son,* concurs and appreciates Matt's cool-headed-ness. "Matt's got one thing that is rare and important—he's disciplined," said Dennehy to *Daily Variety.* "He has controls, brakes, and he's unusual in that. We're all too familiar with James Dean wanna-bes and that's definitely not where Matt's at. His self-control makes him different in a town that sometimes rewards bad behavior."

Matt seems to understand the detrimental effects that a big ego can have on your career as well as your work ethic. He thinks that Marlon Brando "has done more to destroy this generation of actors," than any other performer. This is not because he thinks Brando is a less than exceptional actor. On the contrary, he respects the actor greatly and blames peoples' perception of Brando's "I-don't-give-a-bleep mentality. . . . What people overlook is that when the dude was my age, he was the hardest-working man in show business. . . . He was obsessed with acting. When people say, 'I just want to be fat and live in Fiji and have everyone tell me I'm a genius,' they're not looking at what it actually takes to get there," Matt said to *Vanity Fair*.

Though the media can't seem to get enough of Matt right now—his face has graced the covers of at least three major magazines: *Vanity Fair, Interview,* and *Entertainment Weekly* (the last two with Ben)—he knows to take the hype with a grain of salt and just keep the focus on growing as a serious actor. Plus he doesn't put himself in the same "hot" category as Leonardo DiCaprio or Brad Pitt, and he understands that "it could all blow over by this time next year. I won't be Matthew McConaughey," he said to *Vanity Fair*. "I'm not as good-looking as him. I'm certainly never going to be anyone's sex symbol." (McConaughey is certainly an apt comparison: Not only are they both young Hollywood heartthrobs, but they were also both

picked by Steven Spielberg to act in his films. It
doesn't end there. They also both played characters
in films based on John Grisham novels and both
actors' faces ended up on the covers of *Interview*
and *Vanity Fair* about one year apart.)

Some of his fans would beg to differ about that
sex symbol status, but Matt says that that's not
what he's about. His goal is to try to maintain some
degree of normalcy in his life, as well as to have a
successful career. In fact, he thinks that actor Ed
Harris (*Abyss, The Right Stuff*) has the ultimate life
for the simple reason that he's a well-respected
actor who's not overpaid or stalked by a loony and
can lead a semi-normal existence. Besides, Matt
doesn't really like Hollywood's hype and considers
all the attention "weird." He actually sees himself
as an "East Coast person" and plans to settle down
back in his hometown of Boston someday.

Matt's groundedness might come from having
learned the ropes of the biz gradually over a period
of ten years, unlike some under-thirty stars who are
forced, ready or not, into the spotlight overnight.
Though he's younger than most to have such huge
success and stardom (not to mention an Oscar), he
had heard it all before that his star was about to
take off. After such films as *School Ties* and *Courage Under Fire*, industry folk guaranteed Matt that
his career was about to explode. As he told the
Boston Globe: "It just seems so speculative. It
seems like there's no way to really gauge what's real
and what isn't, and if it's going to stay this way. I've
had a couple of false starts with *School Ties* and

Geronimo," after which people told him "Oh, your life's about to change," and nothing did. He's even said that he's a little cynical this time around about his success.

He's not so cynical (or too busy), though, to volunteer his valuable time in the fight against AIDS. In February 1998, Matt added his name to help generate support for the annual Boston AIDS walk, which takes place in June and raises thousands of dollars for AIDS research. By saying yes, Matt made good on a promise he had made a few years ago to Larry Kessler, the executive director of the AIDS Action Committee. During a dinner Kessler had with him, Matt told Kessler that "if there's ever anything I can do to help the cause, let me know." So, Kessler took him up on his offer. Though Matt probably won't be joining the walkers, he did write a letter that was sent out to all past AIDS-walk participants encouraging them to get out there again. "We must not confuse hope with victory," wrote Matt. "The potential to be truly victorious in the battle against AIDS will never be realized if we allow our progress to lull us into complacency."

Ultimately, Matt's attitude and treatment of others could be summed up with reference to what he and Ben tried to do when writing *Hunting.* "A lot of things were important to us writing this script: just treating people nice, not having regrets in the world, being responsible in your relationships, and the way you treat other people. That's our philosophy, basically the Golden Rule."

Looks like Nancy and Kent did a good job.

9

LIBRA GUY

Born on October 8, Matt's keeping good company with other celebrity Libras who share his birthday, such as Sigourney Weaver (*Alien* films), Chevy Chase (*National Lampoon's Vacation*), and Paul Hogan (who's famous for his Crocodile Dundee character). He shares with them the classic Libra trait of a strong imagination, which Matt started revealing from the time he was two when he ran around his house with a blue towel tied around his neck.

Those born on October 8 often derive their wisdom from life experience, which they value more than anything else. This feature of Matt's personality was certainly borne out in the writing of *Good Will Hunting,* through his relationships, such as those with Skylar (Minnie) and Chuckie (Ben), and through his experiences in Boston and at Harvard. He says that even the character of Sean McGuire

(Robin) was based on his relationship with his high school drama teacher, Gerry Speca. A Libra's happiness and stability is directly related to his ability to remain true to his inner self. It's been rumored that Matt was asked if he wanted to be a Calvin Klein underwear model, but Matt's not one to exploit himself nor will he degrade his profession. (Not that anyone would mind seeing Matt clad in only a pair of Calvin Klein skivvies!)

Because Matt was born in the fall, and is ruled under the planet of Venus, he is a very social person and counts friendships and communal activities as being very important. This could explain his large group of friends, and his long-standing friendship with Ben. They also have highly developed people skills and inspire trust in people because they aren't interested in others' misfortunes. Matt said in a Filmscouts.com interview that he was always rooting for Ben, even when they both would be up for the same part.

Libras are often extremely outspoken and usually don't beat around the bush when giving their opinion. And they usually earn respect for their sense of fairness and justice. (Their symbol is the scales after all). Also, autumn people are socially conscious and interested in giving back to their community, and could be the reason that Matt volunteered for the Boston AIDS walk in June 1998.

Appropriately, Libras, more so than the other zodiac signs, often have fit, well-proportioned bodies. One good look at a shirtless Matt torso should convert any non-believers. They are usually in great shape, and they work hard to maintain and improve their appearance, sometimes even to the point of obsession. Matt told Filmscouts.com that the person who had outlined the diet for him to lose forty pounds for *Courage Under Fire* didn't expect him to stick to it, but when he did, people started to worry about him, and rightly so, being that he was on medication to correct his body for two years after that.

Matt seems to be the typical Libra guy, who is usually described as one part boyish charmer, one part Adonis (a beautiful Greek god), and one part ladykiller. Libras are almost always in a relationship, because their sign rules partnerships and marriage, so they never actually see themselves as completely single, and probably haven't quite ended one relationship as another one begins. Judging from Matt's dating patterns, he fits this description perfectly. Not only do they tend to overlap from one relationship to the next, they always seem to be keeping an eye out for the next new version (Winona, take heed).

Libras are always attracted to the latest hot thing, which could explain Matt's attraction to the models and Claire, Minnie, and Winona, but they're not necessarily players—they're usually looking for love, even a relationship, and sometimes just want what others want. But Libras, who melt with compliments, love the courtship stage of a relationship but hate a partner who shows her desperate longings.

Some of Matt's recent dates have been an Aries (Claire), an Aquarius (Minnie), and a Scorpio (his current flame, Winona). Claire's Aries sign is represented by the Ram, a sort of bullish, "I am right" personality. The Libra, though, can usually turn a female Ram into a gentle lamb. But their opposite Zodiac spectrum of fire and air signs could have caused their imminent demise after the wrap of *The Rainmaker*. Or perhaps, because of a Libra's charming ability to attract many adoring fans, Claire's Mars-based sign could have been teaming with jealousy, something not attractive to Libras. However you interpret it, more than anything it was probably his kindness and friendliness that attracted Claire to Matt, and it was probably the same for him.

Though Matt and Minnie seemed to hang tight for longer than he and Claire, it could have been Minnie's Aquarian stubbornness and Matt's Libran bossiness that drove them apart. But you don't have to look far to see what attracted them to each other, because Aquarians and Libras, as did Minnie and Matt, share the common interests of travel, higher education, and the arts. And, who knows, Matt may have been simply drawn to Minnie's Aquarian lovable and fascinating self.

Things look good for Winona and Matt so far, and that could be attributed to the fact that Scorpios are loyal, honorable, and appreciate a Libra's sense of fairness. Scorpios also enjoy a Libra's romantic and affectionate nature. And Scorpio women seem to be able to balance a Libra's scales, by saying the right things and by being patient (should Matt's mood change for the worse). But Matt should watch out and not think he can pull one over on Winona, because a Scorpio woman knows when she's being fooled.

Unfortunately for Matt, the Libra sign is the hardest of all signs to match romantically. The Libra is constantly weighing a potential partner's good and bad qualities and is forever looking for that perfect mate. Couple this trait with the precarious nature of Hollywood love lives, and it should set the stage for lots of girlfriends for Matt and lots of gossip for everyone else.

10

LOOKING FORWARD

For Matt, the last half of 1998 will be a sea of camera crews, wardrobe people tucking and pulling at him, and old buddies, as well as new faces. He has no place to call home at the moment, only "crash pads," such as his mom's new house in Somerville, Massachusetts, or his friend Cole Hauser's place in Los Angeles. The most permanent part of his life right now may be his storage unit in New Jersey.

But housing is not one of Matt's priorities at the moment, nor is it something he has much time to think about. He's waited a long time for this success, this chance to finally put his talents to work on a regular basis for people who really care about a good story and good filmmaking. It's a theme in his life. It's about passion, energy, and fun. It's about seizing the opportunities and doing your very best, not getting jaded, egotistical, or self-conscious. "This whole 'I'm too cool to care' thing you get among young actors in this country is so weak and stupid and played out," Matt said to one interviewer. "It just brings everybody down. You shouldn't be too cool to care. You should be full of vim and vigor, and trying to do everything you can to make a change."

In his young life he's already accomplished more in the acting world than most people twice his age. And in so doing, he's set a new standard, not only for his do-it-yourself attitude as a writer, but as a committed actor, too. It's almost as if he embodies a sort of old-school aesthetic when it comes to acting. He's manic about perfecting his characters, putting enormous amounts of energy into getting them just right. He's not interested in just playing himself or a kid his own age; he wants to be challenged, and he rises to those challenges. On top of all this he's incredibly generous to his colleagues, an actor's actor. This quality will only make other actors jump at the opportunity to work with him when he decides to pursue his next big goal: directing.

For these reasons, and many more, his future looks bright but complicated. For Matt, looking forward is also about learning how to deal with big success: the paparazzi, the interviews, and the money. It's a whole new kind of world, one that is impossible to prepare for, but Matt's got a small army of friends and family who know him, and whom he trusts and can help him cope. Ultimately, though, Matt's too grounded to become something other than what he has been all along: a talented guy who really likes to just hang out with his buddies, play some pick-up basketball, and tell a great story.

11

MATT'S WEB WORLD

With the steady rise of cool Web sites over the last
few years, fans are no longer simply content with
being a part of a fan club or writing letters to their
favorite star. They are more and more showing
their love for their celeb of choice by creating a
Web page dedicated to him or her. This is no
different for Matt Damon. For Matt, though, this is
a recent phenomenon. It's only been in the last year
or so that pages have popped up in his honor. Most
fans took notice of him in 1992's *School Ties,* but it
wasn't until *Courage Under Fire* came out in 1996
that people switched from standard fans ("Yeah,
he's pretty cute . . .") to true devotees ("Oh, my
gosh, I love him. He's the best actor ever on the
planet."). *The Rainmaker* was the clincher, and
soon thereafter Web pages began springing up with
tons of pics, stories, news, and trivia. But, be
forewarned, not everything you read on the Inter-

net is true; many Webmasters try to outdo each other, which can result in stretching the truth. In the following list you will find info on some of the better Matt Damon sites as well as sites that write about the latest in the entertainment and film world.

Just a word of caution, however. Be smart and safe when you surf. Some of these sites have Web chat or posting areas; these can be great areas to exchange info or thoughts with other Matt fans, but don't give out any personal information about yourself in these areas. For one thing, you could start getting SPAM (Internet junk mail) for the rest of your life, which is just plain annoying. But most of all, there's simply no need for anyone else to know your personal info.

Also, Web sites come and go with alarming frequency. Often they're just down for an hour or two, other times they change their Web address and sometimes they just go away altogether. Thus, some of the addresses listed here may not be the latest by the time you read this.

1) THE UNOFFICIAL MATT DAMON PAGE

http://www.geocities.com/Hollywood/Studio/1635

The Unofficial Matt Damon Page is probably the most comprehensive of the Matt Damon Web sites, especially if you're looking for pictures and gossip.

It has TONS of pictures of Matt, great transcripts of interviews, a rumors page, a copy of his college photograph, a survey for Web site guests, a FAQ (frequently asked questions) section, a chat room, and even a space for fans to submit their poems about Matt. Depending on your browser, the only drawback to this well-kept and extensive homage to Matt Damon is the annoying "sponsors" box that sometimes appears when you enter the site. But, hey, it's not cheap to keep up a Web site.

2) GOOD MATT DAMON

http://www.goodmattdamon.com

When you cruise the Good Matt Damon site, you're offered the chance to take part in a weekly poll on an ever-changing Matt Damon topic. Results from the previous week's poll are displayed when you answer the new question. Some of the previous polls asked what type of movie would you most like to see Matt in (result: a drama) and what is your favorite Matt movie (winner: *The Rainmaker*). The well-designed site includes a long biography section, a FAQ section, about 20 magazine articles on Matt, regularly updated Matt news, a photogallery, and a section on the awards Matt has won. There's also a space to subscribe to an online newsletter about Matt called "Planet Damon."

3) JK's MATT DAMON GALLERY

http://www.silverweb.com/JK/matt.htm

With great photographs from magazines, movie stills, and public appearances, this qualifies as one of the top three of the Matt Damon–devoted sites. It also contains a roundup of the films, TV appearances, magazine spreads, and public appearances made by Matt. Also notable: a survey for Web site guests on a variety of topics, including Matt's hairstyle and the film roles he chooses. The only real drawback to this site is that the biography section is currently very brief, although the site manager promises an update to the section soon.

4) DOUBLE TROUBLE

http://members.aol.com/SunsetTea/MattAndBen.html

For those of you who are equally interested in news about both Matt Damon and Ben Affleck, check out this site. It contains bios of each actor, news about their upcoming projects, gossip, pictures from their public appearances, a "VCR Alert" that tells you when to set your recorder for Matt and Ben's next scheduled TV appearances, and a pretty decent selection of articles from magazines. This site is well maintained, and is therefore a good source for recent information.

5) DAVID'S MATT DAMON PAGE

http://members.aol.com/hotdamon/mattdamo.htm

If you like reading about what it's like to meet Matt in person, this site has a great "True Stories About Meeting Matt" section. Also, if you have a tale about running into the Blond One, you can add it to the list. In addition to Matt's bio and film info, there's a future and current film section and some recent interview transcripts from the Mr. Showbiz Web site.

6) VIEW ASKEW

http://www.viewaskew.com

Though this site is dedicated to indie-film director Kevin Smith, you'll find a lot of current newsy facts (and photos) about Matt and Ben because they are starring in Kevin's next film, *Dogma*. If you check out their News Askew section, you're sure to find the latest updates on the film and whatever rumors are floating around about Matt and Ben. They even link you to bio and future-film info on the boys. And every once in a while, Kevin brings in some of his stars to do a Web chat. This actually happened unexpectedly in March, and fans were able to post many questions to which both Matt and Ben spent about two hours answering honestly and thoughtfully.

7) AIN'T IT COOL NEWS

http://www.aint-it-cool-news.com

Maintained by twenty-six-year-old Harry Knowles, who lives in Austin, Texas, this site is dedicated to all things movie-related. Knowles is somewhat famous in the movie and Web world, and was even featured in the April 1998 "Hollywood" issue of *Vanity Fair* for his insider sneak-previews of upcoming movies. Rather than focusing on the love lives of celebrities, Knowles puts his energy into reporting the latest on scripts, casting, pre- and postproduction of films, test screenings, and movie releases. You can bet that Knowles will probably have some of the first reviews of Matt's upcoming films.

8) MR. SHOWBIZ

http://www.mrshowbiz.com

An extension of *ABC News,* this well-designed site covers not only movie and celebrity happenings, but music news as well. With a long list of contributing writers who write for such publications as *The Village Voice,* New York's *Daily News,* and many alternative mags across the country, this site's news and interviews are always current and well-written. It also has a great search feature that allows you to look up past info and articles on Matt, as well as his bio and filmography.

9) PEOPLE ONLINE

http://www.pathfinder.com/
or **www.people.com**

If you don't subscribe to *People* magazine, or just forgot to pick up a copy at the newsstand, this is a great alternative to the weekly printed version. Not only do you get most of the magazine's content, but you're also able to access the online stuff, which is separate from the magazine and often contains new and interesting facts about Matt, or other celebrity faves. Plus the site is updated daily, so you can get your up-to-the-minute celeb fix.

10) E! ONLINE

http://www.eonline.com

E! Online is the companion site to E! Television. It is updated daily and rivals Mr. Showbiz with its offerings of the latest in entertainment news, and though the design isn't as cool-looking as Mr. Show-biz's, the celeb stories are timely and well-written. E!'s gossip section is always chock full of juicy tidbits, and Matt's goings-on are consistently reported here.

GOOD MATT FACTS

1. Matt made a pilgrimage to French Lick, Indiana, just so he could visit the home town of legendary Boston Celtic basketball player Larry Bird.
2. In *Good Will Hunting,* MIT is shown with lockers in its hallways. The real MIT doesn't have any lockers on campus, anywhere.
3. Matt used to break dance in Harvard Square, in Cambridge, Massachusetts, for extra money.
4. *Tender Mercies,* starring Robert Duvall, is one of Matt's all-time favorite movies.
5. In *Hunting,* Professor Lambeau's first name is Gerry, and his assistant's name is Tom. Matt and Ben created the "Tom and Gerry" names as an inside joke referring to the cartoon cat and mouse, Tom and Jerry.
6. Matt's favorite movie of 1997 was Ang Lee's

The Ice Storm. Incidentally, that also happened to be Minnie's fave for 1997, too.

7. Matt's favorite actors are Robert Duvall, Morgan Freeman, Robert DeNiro, and the Pink Panther, Peter Sellars.

8. *Good Will Hunting* surpassed Miramax's former top box office seller, *Pulp Fiction,* when it topped one-hundred-twenty-million dollars in the U.S. (Not a bad profit—the film only cost about ten mil to make.)

9. Matt wore rocks in his suit during a tense trial scene in *The Rainmaker* to make himself feel uncomfortable so that his character would look even more tense.

10. *Good Will Hunting* was nominated for nine Oscars; it won two: one for Best Original Screenplay, and one for Best Supporting Actor.

11. Matt was sixteen when he told his parents he wanted to be a professional actor, and, with Ben's help, he flew to New York and got an agent.

12. Matt's first movie role was as Steamer in *Mystic Pizza,* which starred Julia Roberts and Lili Taylor. He had only one line.

13. Matt and Ben wrote *Good Will Hunting* because they weren't finding any good parts that they liked.

14. Matt and Ben met when they were ten and eight, respectively. They grew up two blocks apart.

15. In a bar scene in *Good Will Hunting,* Minnie's character, Skylar, tells a joke to Will's gang

that cracks them up. But that joke is different from the one in the original script. The original joke was about an Irish guy getting granted three wishes, and for all three he asks for never-ending pints of Guiness (Irish beer).

16. Ben says Matt's pretty much a slob around the house and has many stories to tell about Matt casually hanging out in the middle of month-old food containers.

17. Before Matt and Ben came along, Patrick Ewing, star center of the New York Knicks basketball team, was the most famous alumnus of Cambridge Rindge and Latin high school.

18. Matt's Aunt Diane used to baby-sit Jay Leno.

19. The first day of shooting *Hunting,* Matt and Ben started crying because their dream was finally coming true.

20. Matt's mom, Nancy, worries about the effects that fame and fortune will have on her son.

21. Matt says he took the role of Private Ryan in Steven Spielberg's next film, *Saving Private Ryan,* because, well, Spielberg asked him to.

22. When Matt and Ben are hanging out, Ben usually drives; he was usually the typist, too, when he and Matt were writing *Good Will Hunting.*

23. Matt lost the role of Alan Isaacman in *The People vs. Larry Flynt* to Edward Norton, and Edward lost the role of Rudy Baylor in *The Rainmaker* to Matt; now the two are working together in the poker drama *Rounders.*

24. Even though they're both from Boston and

some people think they look just like brothers, Matt is not related to fellow Bostonian actor Mark Wahlberg (Marky Mark).

25. Matt's opening line for his college essay to Harvard was, "For as long as I can remember, I've wanted to be an actor."

26. Matt's first year at Harvard, he auditioned for Disney's *Mickey Mouse Club;* apparently he wasn't Mouseketeer material, he didn't get a part.

27. In the *Hunting* scene where Robin Williams is talking to Matt about his deceased wife's propensity for farting, Matt and Robin are truly laughing because Robin was ad-libbing (making it up as he went along). The original scene has Robin's character, Sean, talking about how his wife would turn off his alarm in the middle of the night, making him late for work.

28. Matt lost twenty pounds just to *audition* for a part in Gus Van Sant's *To Die For.* The role went to Joaquin Phoenix.

29. When Matt was a tyke, he lived in Newton, Massachusetts, next door to author/historian Howard Zinn, who wrote the book *A People's History of the United States.* Matt had to read the book in high school for history teacher Larry Aaronson. And in *Hunting,* Matt's character Will recommends the book to Robin's Sean, as a great read.

30. After getting so good while practicing for their roles in the poker movie *Rounders,* Matt and

Edward Norton may compete in a real life, heavy duty professional poker playoff at a Las Vegas casino.

31. In *Good Will Hunting,* Matt's Will makes fun of Robin Williams' therapist Sean about his painting of a man lost at sea in the middle of a bad storm. The painting was actually made by *Hunting*'s director, Gus Van Sant.

32. If you look carefully in the Au Bon Pain scene in *Good Will Hunting,* where Matt's Will describes his particular brand of smarts to Minnie's Skylar, you can spot Matt's and Ben's families and friends at surrounding tables. At one table is Matt's dad, Kent, playing chess with Matt's surrogate father, Jay Jones; at an adjacent table is one of Matt's high school teachers, Larry Aaronson, sitting with Matt's and Ben's moms.

33. Gus Van Sant and singer-songwriter Elliott Smith, whose song "Miss Misery" was nominated for Best Song at the 1998 Academy Awards, are acquaintances from their home town of Portland, Oregon.

Matt Trivia

1. What do Matt's friends and family affectionately call him?

2. How old were Matt and Ben when they met?

3. How many Oscar nominations did *Good Will Hunting* get?

4. How many actual Oscars did it win?

5. How many Oscars did Matt win?

6. How long did it take Matt and Ben to get *Good Will Hunting* to the silver screen?

7. How old was Matt when he started acting?

8. How old was Matt's Will Hunting character?

9. What was Matt's first film?

10. What was his first commercial?

11. How many pounds did Matt lose for the Ilario role in *Courage Under Fire?*

12. What's Matt's brother's name?

13. How much older than Matt is he?

14. True or false: Matt's brother is also an actor.

15. Where did Matt grow up?

16. True or false: Matt's eyes are brown.

17. What college did Matt go to?

18. True or false: Matt graduated from college in 1992.

19. How tall is Matt: (a) 5'8" (b) 5'10" (c) 6'0"

20. How did Matt break his ankle at four years old?

21. What's the name of the burger joint where Will and Skylar have their first date in *Hunting?*

22. When will Matt be twenty-eight?

23. True or false: *Good Will Hunting* started out as an action-adventure film?

24. For what upcoming film project will Matt lose another twenty pounds?

25. What was the first film that Matt and Ben appeared in together?

26. Who did Matt and Ben forget to thank when they won their Oscars?

27. What was Matt's worst date?

28. When did Claire Danes and Matt start dating?

29. True or false: Claire and Matt dated longer than he and Minnie.

30. What's the next film that Matt and Ben will star in together?

31. How old was Matt when he got his first agent?

32. Who did Matt claim, "put a smokin' on me," in reference to his losing the lead part in *Primal Fear*.

33. True or false: Matt's favorite movie as a kid was *Saturday Night Fever*.

ANSWERS TO QUIZ

1. Matty

2. Matt, ten, and Ben, eight

3. Nine nominations

4. Two Oscars

5. One Oscar

6. Five years

7. Twelve years old

8. Twenty years old

9. *Mystic Pizza*

10. T. J. Maxx

11. Forty pounds

12. Kyle

13. Three years

14. False, he's a sculptor

15. Boston, Massachusetts

16. False, they're blue

17. Harvard

18. False, he went through ceremonies, but he still hasn't graduated

19. (b) 5'10"

20. He jumped from a jungle gym

21. The Tasty

22. October 8, 1998

23. True

24. *The Talented Mr. Ripley*

25. *School Ties*

26. Kevin Smith

27. His senior prom

28. On the set of *The Rainmaker*

29. False

30. *Dogma*

31. Sixteen years old

32. Edward Norton

33. False. It was everyone else's favorite, *Star Wars.*

ABOUT THE AUTHOR

Maxine Diamond is a freelance writer living in New York City. She writes about a number of topics, including theater, dance, the Internet, and sports.

THE HOTTEST STARS
THE BEST BIOGRAPHIES

☆ **Hanson: MMMBop to the Top** ☆
By Jill Mattthews

☆ **Hanson: The Ultimate Trivia Book!** ☆
By Matt Netter

☆ **Isaac Hanson: Totally Ike!** ☆
By Nancy Krulik

☆ **Taylor Hanson: Totally Taylor!** ☆
By Nancy Krulik

☆ **Zac Hanson: Totally Zac!** ☆
By Matt Netter

☆ **Jonathan Taylor Thomas:
Totally JTT!** ☆
By Michael-Anne Johns

☆ **Leonardo DiCaprio: A Biography** ☆
By Nancy Krulik

☆ **Will Power!
A Biography of Will Smith** ☆
By Jan Berenson

☆ **Prince William:
The Boy Who Will Be King** ☆
By Randi Reisfeld

Available from Archway Paperbacks
Published by Pocket Books

1491